THE FIRE BETWEEN US

AND OTHER DARK LOVE STORIES

SHIRLEY SIATON

THE FIRE BETWEEN US
And Other Dark Love Stories

Copyright © 2026 Shirley Siaton Parabia

ALL RIGHTS RESERVED.
No part of this book may be reproduced or used in any manner without the prior written permission of the copyright owner, except for the use of brief quotations in a book review. To request permission, contact the publisher at books@inkysword.com.

This is a work of fiction. Names, characters, businesses, events, and incidents are the products of the author's imagination. Any resemblance to actual persons, living or dead, or actual events is purely coincidental.

All brand and product names used in this book are trademarks, registered trademarks, or trade names of their respective owners. Inky Sword Book Publishing is not associated with any product or vendor in this book.

ISBN 978-1-961052-30-7 (paperback, romance)
ISBN 978-621-490-171-5 (paperback, discreet)

1st Edition, January 2026

Published by Shirley S. Parabia
Romance cover by Angeline Cantila
Discreet cover by Artscandare Book Design
Interior formatting by Champagne Book Design

Inky Sword Book Publishing
Barangay Quezon, Arevalo, Iloilo City 5000
Republic of the Philippines

inkysword.com

A NOTE FOR THE READER

Thank you for picking up *The Fire Between Us and other dark love stories*. As the title suggests, this collection walks the fine line between passion and destruction. These stories explore the raw, unpolished, and often dangerous sides of romance. They feature morally grey heroes, intense obsessions, and characters who find love in the shadows.

While I believe deeply in the catharsis and resilience found within these pages, I want you to be able to make the best and safest reading choice for you. Your mental well-being is the most important thing.

Please be aware that this collection contains the following themes and potential triggers:

- Explicit sexual content (spice)
- Kidnapping and abduction
- Non-consensual drugging/sedation
- Stalking and obsessive behavior
- Grief, bereavement, and the death of a spouse/fiancé
- Recounted suicide and death of a parent
- Vigilante justice, prison, and revenge killing
- Physical violence, blood, and injuries (on page)
- Attempted mugging and assault
- Mentions of cancer and fatal car accidents
- Natural disasters (flooding and storms)
- Dubious consent and power imbalance dynamics

To Peter

Through the fire

Within, and after

I am yours

CONTENTS

THE FIRE
BETWEEN US

CHAPTER 1

THE GARDEN

THE SOUND OF HIS VOICE RIPPLES THROUGH THE QUIET of the garden.

"Viv? Something wrong?"

A shiver runs through me as a gust of wind unsettles the warm summer evening, rustling the bougainvillea and making the air feel suddenly cooler. I close my eyes, lean back in the rocking chair, and let the darkness after sunset press against me like a blanket.

The crickets are singing again, steady and endless, and for a moment I pretend that's all there is—the song, the night, the slow creak of wood beneath me.

The garden has always been my sanctuary. My mother's roses, the scent of soil and old earth, the way shadows bend in the corners but never quite threaten. I've lost hours here, lulled by the familiar.

But tonight the calm feels fragile. Too easily broken.

"Viv?"

His hand lands gently on my arm, warm against my skin.

I open my eyes, push a stray strand of hair from my face, and look at him at last.

Lloyd.

He's been standing here for minutes, maybe more, watching me. Always watching. I wonder if he has guessed what I've been thinking.

How heavy the world feels. Or how brittle I am beneath the surface.

"Hi." My voice comes out softer than I want it to. "I thought you'd be packing for tomorrow's flight."

I stretch slowly, forcing myself into movement, forcing a smile. "It leaves early. And don't think you're skipping my Bon Voyage breakfast. You promised."

He smiles back, his brown eyes glinting like they carry some secret light of their own. Lloyd is handsome in a way that makes people look twice. Dark hair falling around his temples, profile carved in a classic kind of way, a face that would have been at home in an old black-and-white Sampaguita Pictures movie.

And yet, he doesn't belong here. Not in my quiet garden, not in this small town he'd long since outgrown.

"Your breakfast offer is something no sane man would refuse," he teases.

I snort and look away before he can read too much in my expression. "Flatterer."

But he doesn't let it go. He never does.

"What's wrong, Viv?" His voice is gentler now, but more insistent too. "Is something wrong?"

He's more sensitive than I give him credit for. He always has been.

"I haven't eaten much today," I admit, though it's only part of the truth. "Migraine. Takes the appetite away."

He studies me, then slips an arm around my shoulders. I let him, even though the weight of his arm feels both safe and suffocating. "You look pale. Come over to the house. My cousins brought a feast—*lechon, talaba*, the works. I came to see if you'd join us."

I shake my head. "Do you mind if I stay here a while?"

"No. Not at all."

So I rest my head against his shoulder anyway, my body betraying me. For a moment the pain in my skull eases, the scent of his cologne familiar and comforting. He hasn't changed it since college.

Then he clears his throat. "So, Viv."

Something in his tone makes me lift my head. He won't look me in the eyes.

"I hope things are okay with you," he says, too quickly. "You've got to take care of yourself. Tita Roma told me you stay up until dawn, drink coffee like water."

"I work better at night. You know that." My arms fold around me before I even think, shielding myself.

He sighs, then reaches for my hand. I pull it away.

"We're all concerned," he tries again. "Slow down. Don't be too hard on yourself."

"I like my work." My voice takes on an edge. The air between us turns brittle.

"Easy, Viv." He raises his hands like he's surrendering. "I don't want you angry at me for caring about you."

The words slam into me harder than they should.

Caring about you.

I don't let myself believe them. Not when belief could unravel me.

Lloyd has always cared. He's been there with the chocolates on my birthday, the flowers, the ridiculous cartoon cards that made me laugh when no one else could. His sudden return to my life this week has left me off balance, a strange mix of comfort and disquiet. He's been beside me every day, prying open the quiet corners I've built around myself.

"Please," he says. "Don't be mad."

I sigh. I can't fight him, not when he won't fight back. "I'm sorry. Migraines make me cranky."

"Don't apologize." He draws me close again, firmer this time, and presses a kiss against the side of my head.

It's a brotherly gesture. It always has been. We grew up like this. Same street, same schools, our mothers tied by grief and friendship as young widows. He's always been the boy next door, the one who never made me feel small even as he outpaced me in everything else.

I should resent him, but I don't.

Earlier this week, I let him read my draft pitches. He praised them with such sincerity it had left me stunned. Two days later, I was speaking with his editor on the phone, a woman with a kind, smooth voice who told me she was impressed with my samples.

Lloyd had done that. Without asking. Without warning.

Just like that, he had shifted the axis of my world.

But change has always scared me.

Because if he could step in and alter my life so easily, he could just as easily step out again.

And I would be left alone once more, in distance and silence.

CHAPTER 2

THE PARK

SHE'S ICE.

Not the Vivian I grew up with, the one who laughed too loud and argued with me over nothing just to win. Not the girl who scribbled poems in the margins of our journalism notes. Tonight she's quiet, withdrawn, her words clipped like she's holding them hostage.

And it cuts me.

Because being with her is the only part of this week that has felt real. The reason I traded two big stories, the reason I let my producer's messages go to voicemail, the reason I've ignored the little notes that keep slipping into my inbox.

We know where you live.

Stop writing.

Even the death threats feel distant here, in her garden.

in her presence. But Viv, shutting herself off like this…that I can't handle.

I don't want to leave her in this state. Hell, I don't want to leave her at all.

"Why don't we go somewhere," I say, aiming for lightness, like old times. "I don't think I can stomach another bite of *lechon* if I want to run the marathon again."

Her shoulders tense. She pulls away, just enough for me to feel the loss.

Did I say something wrong? Do something? I replay the whole week in my head, every smile she gave me, every silence I filled, and I come up empty.

She hesitates. "Okay. But we need to be back before midnight. You know how our moms are."

Relief sparks in my chest. "The park, then?"

"Okay. Give me a minute. I'll meet you outside."

She slips into the house, leaving me with the echo of her absence.

I head next door, where the cousins are still raising hell. Someone's butchering 'Closer You and I' by Gino Padilla on the videoke, and the table's a mess of pork bones and empty oyster shells.

I grab my mother's car keys. "I'm driving out."

"You mean Lloyd's got a hot night with his girlfriend!" one of my cousins sings into the mic.

Catcalls erupt, whistles following me out the door. My face burns. If Vivian heard that, she'd kill me on the spot.

I make a mental note to ban them all from the house forever.

When I pull up to the gate, there she is. She's changed

into jeans and a yellow blouse, hair loose and neatly combed, bag slung over her shoulder. The sight of her steals my breath for a second.

I back the car out quickly before the cousins notice her. She'd hate their attention, and she'd take it out on me.

We're on the coastal road in minutes. The night stretches wide and endless, the sea hidden but near. I glance at her. She's stiff, staring out the window, like she'd rather be anywhere but here.

"Remember when we used to take this car to the *arroz caldo* place?" I ask, trying to catch her smile.

Her lips twitch. "All night café. Too bad it closed down. Nobody makes chicken soup like that anymore."

"I remember," I say. "We'd pool our coins and split a serving."

Finally, she looks at me, her mouth softening into the smallest smile. "And split the egg. Yellow for me, white for you."

I laugh. "Still can't eat the yolk because of you."

The silence that follows isn't heavy. It's companionable, the way it used to be when we were younger, scribbling articles and sharing ice cream straight from the tub. I switch on the radio, soft music filling the car as the lights of the park appear ahead.

We pull into the lot. Couples linger under the lamps, families are scattered around the playground, but it's quiet enough. I step out, circle the car, open her door. My instinct is to offer my hand, but I stop myself. She flinched earlier, and the last thing I want is to drive her further into herself.

So I just walk ahead, to the wide stone platform by the

sea. My chest eases when I hear her footsteps falling into place beside mine.

"I wish the rest of the gang were here," I say, pointing at the swings in the middle of the grassy playground. "Louie, Claire, Faye, Dale—they'd be fighting over those seats already."

Her shoulders loosen, the stiffness ebbing. "They have kids who fight over swings now. I saw Louie and his wife in church last month. Three kids. Can you believe it?"

"Maybe more than a few years have passed," I offer.

"Has it really been that long?" Her voice dips wistfully. "It feels like time moves without me. Like everyone's out there living their lives, and I'm stuck."

Her words stab deep. I stop walking. She does too.

What can I say? What can I do?

Then her hand finds mine, cool and trembling.

"I'm sorry," she whispers. "For ruining your last night here. I must sound so depressing."

"No." I squeeze her hand, fragile in mine. "You sound real."

"My problems aren't your problems."

I turn, really looking at her. The moon paints her in silver—dark hair framing her face, eyes more expressive and haunting than she realizes, beauty that aches to look at.

My Viv. Always my Viv.

And there's only one truth left in me.

"I could make them mine."

CHAPTER 3

MY HEART IS A DRUM IN MY CHEST, SO LOUD I'M SURE he can hear it.

I've been wading through dangerous waters all week. Now it feels like I've stumbled into the deep end, where my feet can't touch the ground.

Someone like Lloyd Mosquera isn't supposed to be here, with me.

He's supposed to be out there, on some high-flying assignment for his column and syndicated show *'Man on Fire,'* his byline in bold, his words sparking outrage and debate across the country.

He's supposed to be untouchable. Larger than life. A man made of fire and ink and distance.

Not this real.

Not standing in front of me, with his eyes burning holes through me.

Not close enough to feel like he could rewrite everything I thought I knew about myself.

"You don't know what you're saying, Lloyd," I say, tearing my hand away and wrapping my arms around myself. It's my armor now, my default defense whenever he makes me feel too much.

It was a mistake coming here. I should have stayed in my garden, safe and small.

But Lloyd never lets go. Not in his writing, not in life.

He rounds on me, his voice raw but still controlled. "The least you could do is give me a little credit, Viv. I do know what I'm talking about sometimes."

"You think you know anything about me?" My voice cracks with the frustration boiling under my ribs. "That somehow, after a week, you could just…fix everything?"

His jaw tightens. He doesn't move, but I feel the force of him like a firestorm barely contained. "Is that what you think I want to do? Change your life? Play the hero?" His voice lowers, hotter and rougher this time. "I couldn't change anyone's life, Viv. Least of all yours."

"Then what do you want?" The tears sting, threatening to spill. I hate them. I hate him for pulling them out of me. "What do you want from me?"

His eyes soften, but his body hums with restraint, like he's one wrong word away from breaking. "I want to be in your life. Not to fix it, not to carry it, but just to be there. When you're stuck. When you can't move."

"Why?" My voice cracks like glass.

"You know why."

The words are a whisper, nearly swallowed by the crash of waves against stone. But I hear them. I feel them.

His gaze says the rest.

And something inside me breaks.

My arms fall to my sides. My knees threaten to give way. Breathing is suddenly impossible, because my chest isn't hollow anymore.

It's full. Too full.

Wonder. Disbelief. Heat. Love.

One spark, and I'm burning.

I don't know who moves first.

Him. Me. Both of us.

All I know is that his mouth is on mine, and I'm lost.

Lloyd kisses like he writes. Unyielding, relentless, pouring everything into it until you're drowning in his truth.

His hand buries itself in my hair, tugging me closer, tilting my head so he can claim me deeper. I gasp, and he swallows it whole, his tongue stroking against mine, setting me on fire.

My hands fist in his shirt, pulling him closer, closer still, until my body is pressed against the solid heat of his. He's all muscle, all strength, the scent of salt and him wrapping around me.

I melt, and he devours.

His mouth trails lower, nipping at the corner of my jaw, down the line of my throat. My head falls back, a shudder ripping through me as his lips burn against my skin.

"I hope you know what you're getting yourself into," I breathe.

His breath is hot against my jugular. "I know exactly where I'm meant to be."

And when he pulls back just enough to look at me, his eyes are molten even in the shadows of the platform.

For years I thought I'd lost him to the bigger world, to the bright lights and dangerous shadows he walked through so easily. I thought he'd left me behind.

But here he is.

And here I am.

My body is fire. My mind is static. Everything inside me says too much.

His hands are in my hair, down my back, gripping my waist with a kind of desperation that makes me feel weak and shaky. He catches me, hauling me against him, and I feel the hard, undeniable press of him through his jeans.

Heat floods me. My body aches for him in a way I can't hide.

"Lloyd," I whisper, half a warning, half a plea.

I know we're hidden from the rest of the world by the seawall, but someone could easily walk down from the park and see us.

"Viv." His voice is ragged, breathless. "Tell me to stop and I will."

But I don't. I can't.

Not even with the risk of getting caught.

Instead, I grab his shirt and tug it up, my fingers skimming hot skin as I push it over his head. The sight of him steals my breath.

Moonlight spills on his broad chest, showing muscles tight from years of carrying the weight of his world. A faint scar slices across his ribs like proof of all the danger he never talks about.

"God," I murmur, tracing it before I can stop myself.

He catches my wrist, eyes blazing. "Not now." And then he's kissing me again, harder, his hands sliding under my blouse, palms burning against my bare skin.

I gasp when his thumbs brush the underside of my breasts, when his mouth leaves mine to trail fire down my throat. "Lloyd…"

"I've always wanted you, Viv," he groans against my skin. "Say you want me too."

"I want you." The words break out of me. "I want you, Lloyd."

That's all it takes.

He pushes me gently back against the cold stone wall of the platform, his mouth finding mine again, his hands tugging at my jeans, fumbling at the button until I help him. The air stings against my skin as he slides them down, his touch following.

My hands dive into his hair, pulling him closer as he presses his hips to mine. The friction makes me cry out, the sound lost in his kiss. He's hard and hot, grinding against me in a way that makes my whole body catch fire.

"Here?" I manage, breathless, half in disbelief.

"Here." His voice is breathless. "I can't wait, Viv. I've waited too long."

His hand slips under my panties, and I arch into him, a cry tearing from my throat as his fingers find me, stroke me, tease me. He knows exactly what he's doing, exactly how to unravel me. I cling to him, gasping, shuddering, my body already spiralling out of control.

And when I'm shaking apart in his arms, he whispers against my lips, "I've got you. Always."

I don't remember how his jeans come off, only the sound of the zipper, the rush of cool air, then the heat of him pressing against me. He looks into my eyes, waiting, trembling as hard as I am.

"Yes," I murmur. "Please."

And then he's inside me, filling me, stretching me until I can't breathe. I clutch his shoulders, nails biting into his skin, and he groans like he's breaking.

He thrusts into me, slow at first, then harder, deeper, each movement sending shockwaves through me. My back arches against the stone, my legs wrap tightly around his hips, pulling him closer and deeper.

"Viv," he gasps, burying his face in my neck. "God, Viv…"

"Don't stop," I beg, meeting him, moving with him, the rhythm building between us until it feels like the whole world has narrowed to his body, his breath, his lips whispering my name.

When release tears through me, it's like the sea itself has risen up to swallow me whole. I cry out his name, trembling, clinging to him as he follows me over the edge, his body shaking, his groan muffled against my skin.

We collapse together, tangled and breathless.

"I hope you know what this means," he says, reaching to trace the curve of my cheek.

"I do," I answer, my body still trembling, my heart still racing. "And I don't care."

Because even if his world is dangerous, even if his shadows follow me now, he knows I've chosen him.

And he's chosen me.

CHAPTER 4

THE SHADOWS

S HE'S STILL TREMBLING WHEN I HOLD HER. Her breath shudders against my chest, her body soft and pliant in my arms. I swear I could stay like this forever.

The crash of the sea behind us is steady, but all I hear is her heartbeat against mine.

My Viv.

I've wanted her for so long I almost can't believe she's real in my arms, her skin warm, her lips swollen, her scent and sweat all over me.

"I meant it," I say into her hair, my throat tight. "Every word."

Her fingers graze my jaw, and she looks at me like I'm both a miracle and a mistake. "I know."

The undoing in her eyes is enough to break me.

I should stop. I should protect her from this. I should protect her from me.

But I can't. I won't.

Because I know she's always been mine.

She kisses me again, slowly.

"Again," she says, so soft the sound is almost carried away by the wind.

I freeze. "Say what?"

She giggles, then nibbles at my lower lip and whispers, "Don't you dare hold back now, Mosquera."

"Fuck," I growl as she reaches for my cock, already hard again at her touch.

I lay her down on the cold stone. This time I taste every inch of her, mapping her skin with my mouth. Her blouse rides up, baring her to the night air, and I drag my lips down her chest, her ribs, listening to the way she gasps and arches for me.

"Lloyd…" The sound of my name from her lips nearly kills me.

"I wanna taste you, Viv," I rasp, mouth teasing against her skin, until it finally reaches the wetness between her thighs.

I nip and suck, tongue drawing circles, breath tickling the soft, thin hair that carries her scent of roses and dew.

She lets out a strangled cry, hips buckling. "*Lloyd. Please.*"

I growl against her, my body burning.

Mine.

She's mine now.

When I slide back into her, it's deeper and slower, a claiming as much as a surrender. Her legs tighten around me, and I bury my face against her neck as I move inside her, slow at first, then harder and faster, until we're both coming apart together.

We collapse again, tangled and slick with sweat, her chest rising against mine. I press kisses into her hair, her temple, her mouth, drinking her in to convince myself that everything I ever wanted is now in my arms.

I don't know how long we stay like that. Time feels suspended, caught between her heartbeat and mine.

Eventually, I force myself to say, "We should go."

My chest aches with the words. Leaving feels like cutting a vein open.

She nods reluctantly, and I help her up, smoothing her hair, steadying her when her knees wobble. We laugh quietly at ourselves as we help each other dress, then walk back to the car. My fingers stay twined with hers, unwilling to let go.

But just as I open her door, my phone buzzes. The screen lights up.

Unknown number.

My stomach clenches. I see the message and my jaw locks tight. I shove the phone back into my pocket before she can read the words.

We saw you tonight. Enjoy. We'll be waiting.

"Work?" she asks, her voice soft, almost drowsy.

"Something like that," I mutter, squeezing her hand before I can stop myself. Then I force a smile I don't feel. "Nothing for you to worry about."

But I do worry. Because the shadows I've been keeping at bay just saw the one thing they can use against me.

I slide behind the wheel. Her hand rests on my thigh,

and when I lace my fingers over hers, I swear I'll burn the world before I let anyone touch her.

As we pull away from the park, I know that this is only the beginning.

The beginning of us.

The beginning of whatever storms come with my name.

I can already feel the weight of them pressing closer. Unknown numbers, threats on smuggled notes, whispers from strangers on the street.

They're the kind of enemies who don't stop until they've gutted you.

But tonight I have her hand in mine, her warmth still on my skin, her trust burning in my heart.

I know I'll never let her go. Not this time.

If the world wants a war, it will get one.

Because wherever I go next, whatever shadows rise to meet me, she is coming with me.

A SHADOW HEART

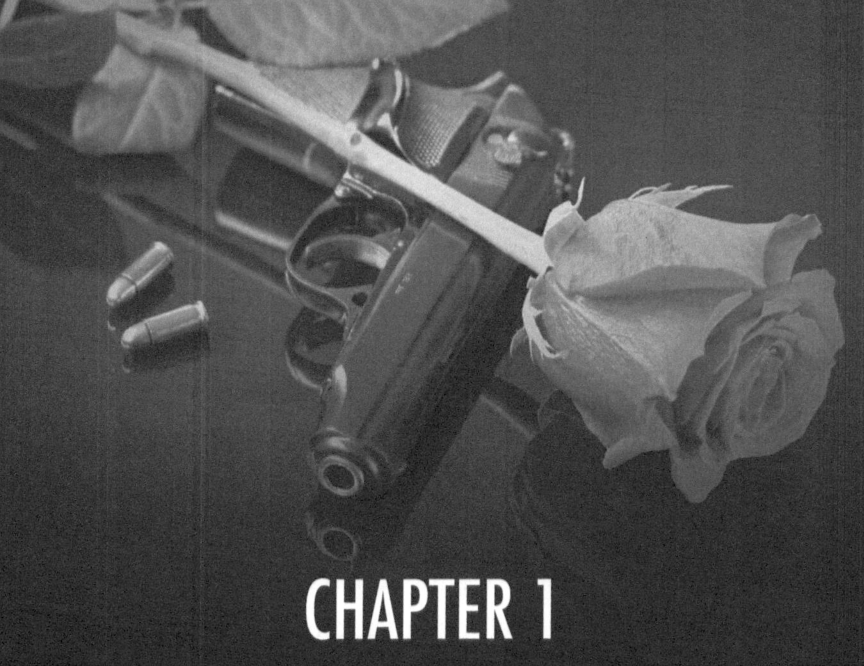

CHAPTER 1

THE LIGHTS

THE LIGHTS ARE TOO BRIGHT.

Not the kind I'm used to—neon signs flickering in seedy motels, or the sterile glow of Makati towers.

These are cheap, borrowed bulbs strung across bamboo poles, their wires sagging, their glow uneven. But it works. The coffee shop looks alive.

Music spills out into the street, a mix of OPM classics and whatever upbeat trash the DJ they hired could cobble together. The banner above the little shop reads *Brew & Break: Coffee for the Puyat Generation.*

It's all clever. And true.

I know I shouldn't be here, but I am.

The job offer hasn't come in yet. No contract. No instructions.

I'm only here to watch. To learn. That's what I tell myself.

But my eyes keep finding her.

Lara Bienvenides. A politician's daughter. A Congressman's pretty little gem. She shouldn't normally be anywhere near this crowd. The coffee shop is filled with a mix of students in uniforms, call center kids still in ID lanyards, and yuppies clutching cheap plastic tumblers like trophies.

But here she is, with her older brother Luke. He owns the place and she works for him. It's not a secret that they have left their parents to strike out on their own. Their father, Lawrence, had been implicated one too many times in misspent pork barrel investigations and disappearing flood control projects, but he's slipped out all of them fairly unscathed.

Lara has the sleeves of her simple white shirt rolled up. Her hair's tied back, a few strands sticking to her forehead with sweat. She's carrying trays of iced coffee and complimentary cookies, laughing with strangers, brushing errant sugar and crumbs off her jeans as moves around the room.

She looks free.

And it makes something twist in my chest.

A group of young men and women invite me to join their table, but I ignore them. I'm leaning against the far wall, shadowed, my usual place wherever I am. I sip the cold bottle of light beer I bought just to blend in.

My mask is off. Not the cloth one, but the mask of distance. Tonight, I let myself watch.

Later, Luke makes a speech. It's nervous and awkward, about dreams and hard work and no shortcuts. The crowd cheers him on. Lara claps the loudest. Her smile is proud, fond, and real.

It doesn't take long before couples take to the tiny space in the middle of the shop, set up as a makeshift dance floor.

Then the music changes to something slow, almost moody. An old Rivermaya song, maybe.

Before I know what I'm doing, I push off the wall.

Lara's near the counter, wiping away sweat from her forehead with a white handkerchief, a small smile of relief on her delicate face. She looks up, startled, when I stop in front of her.

My voice comes out low and steady. Not a request. Not quite a command.

"Dance with me."

CHAPTER 2

"**D**ANCE WITH ME."
The words cut through the noise of the crowd. Not loud or demanding. Just steady, like he knew I'd hear him.

I look up, startled, wiping sweat from my forehead with my handkerchief.

He's a stranger, distinctly taller than most people in the room. He's broad-shouldered, hair swept back from his face and tied neatly, face too angular and sharp-featured to be handsome. A scar cuts across his left cheek.

He's dressed too plainly to be one of Kuya's investors, too clean to be one of the neighborhood kids, too casual to be working at one of the offices nearby. It's just a plain black shirt over some dark jeans.

I should laugh, tell him no. But something in his dark

eyes holds me still. Something deep and unspoken. I feel like they've been on me all night.

And maybe I like that.

So I nod.

His hand closes around mine. It's large and calloused, his grip warm and certain. My pulse jumps.

He draws me into the open space where couples sway to Rivermaya. His other hand settles at my waist, steady, anchoring me in the crush of the crowd.

My body tenses, then softens as he guides me. He's close, close enough that I can feel the heat of him through my sweaty shirt, close enough that his chest brushes mine when we change tempo or angles.

"What's your name?" I ask, because I need words to distract myself from how hard my heart is beating.

"Jace." His voice is deep, slightly raspy at the edges. I imagine it whispering my name, and heat rushes to my face.

"Jace…" I repeat, trying it out. It fits. Strong, short, and dangerous. "I'm Lara."

"I know." His mouth almost curves, like he's smiling at some private joke.

He doesn't smell like anyone else here—not beer, not sweat, not even cologne. Just rain and smoke and something clean that clings to my skin when I breathe him in.

"You don't look like someone who hangs out at coffee shop launches," I murmur.

"First time." His gaze never leaves mine. "Worth it."

"Well, that's nice to hear," I say. "You should visit more often. Support local businesses."

"Maybe I should," he answers softly. "If I get to see you like this."

I blush again, swallowing as I look away.

He doesn't say anything, but his hand on my waist digs a little deeper into the fabric of my shirt, the heat seeping into my skin underneath.

The song is ending.

I don't want it to.

He leans in, close enough that his breath brushes my ear. "Thank you for the dance. Goodnight, Lara."

And then he's gone.

He just lets me go, as if the moment never mattered, and disappears into the night.

I stand frozen in the middle of the crowd, breathless, my skin tingling where he touched it, my heart still racing like I've just stepped off the rooftop of a skyscraper.

Whatever the hell that was…

I'm not walking away from it unchanged.

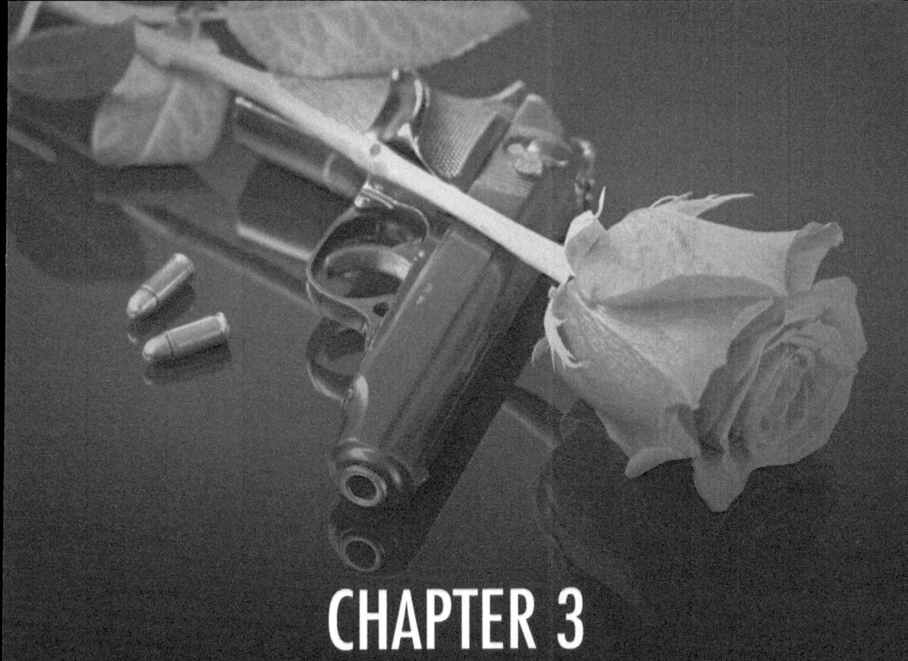

CHAPTER 3

THE JOB

THE BAR SMELLS OF STALE GIN AND WET ASHTRAYS. I don't remember how many times I've been here before, but I know it's always to pick up my end of a contract. My handler likes the place because no one really asks too many questions.

I sit in the corner booth, shadowed and waiting. The woman arrives late—sharp cream suit, a sharper humorless smile, the kind that says she's paid to make problems vanish. She slides a folder across the table without bothering with pleasantries. This will be my third job with their party.

"Jace," she says, voice smooth. "This one's important. A Congressman's daughter. Leverage. Let's just say we want the old man to get off his high horse."

I don't touch the folder yet. I just listen.

"The girl's visible. Loved by the press. Always on her

brother's arm at these little…projects of his. They're trying to build a business empire together, coffee shops and restaurants. A cheap concept, but it makes them accessible, relatable. People like them. Her more so. She's not the usual spoiled rich girl who posts pictures of expensive vacations on social media. She's a college student. All that."

I nod, not saying anything. Politicians don't want their kids to be liked. They want them to be untouchable, just like them. For when the time comes.

"The job is clean," she continues. "Grab her. Hold her. We'll take care of the rest. Price is double your previous fee. We don't want anyone to see or suspect anything. So we got the best in the business for this sort of thing."

I flip the folder open. Photos slide out.

Lara Bienvenides. Up close, in profile, laughing with her brother in front of a coffee cart at Glorietta. Another shot, her in a light dress at some ribbon-cutting event. She looks a bit younger in it.

But it's the same angel of a woman from the party.

Her eyes are just as I remember. Wide, bright, and alive.

I shut the folder before the woman sees too much in my face.

"I'll do it," I say.

"Fifty percent will be wired within the hour," she confirms.

"Make it sixty. I'll let you know when it's time for pick-up." My voice doesn't falter, though my chest feels tight.

She looks at me for a moment, then nods.

"Fine. We'll wait for your call."

In daylight, the coffee shop is small, squeezed between a pawnshop and a convenience store, its new signboard still smelling of paint. Inside, the tables are crowded with students and call center kids nursing cups of cheap caffeine like it's holy water.

I step up to the counter. The menu is handwritten on kraft paper. *Matapang Brew, Puyat Latte, 2AM Americano.*

And then I see her.

She's behind the counter, apron tied around her waist, sleeves rolled up like before. Her thick black hair is in a loose pile at the top of her head. Her skin looks dewy in the soft lights of the shop.

Her brother is in the back arguing with a supplier, and she's running the register herself.

She glances up, and the moment her eyes lock on mine, something clicks into place. Recognition. And wariness. Maybe something else.

For a heartbeat, neither of us speaks.

Then I clear my throat. "Black coffee, please."

She blinks, nods quickly, and turns to pour. The small act—her fingers steady, her hair falling into her face, the steam curling between us—feels louder than the busy chatter of the whole shop.

When she sets the paper cup down between us, our hands almost touch.

"You came back," she says softly.

I wrap my hand around the cup, holding onto the heat. "I said I would. Worth it."

Her lips part, and I see the faintest trace of a smile before she catches herself and looks away.

I turn away without another word, the coffee burning down my throat as I drink it to hide my face.

For the first time in years, the contract feels heavier than the gun under my shirt.

CHAPTER 4

THE WALK

T HE SHOP IS BUSY FOR ANOTHER HOUR OR SO—
students bent over their laptops, workers laughing too
loudly over greasy plates of fries and sliders, young
couples huddled next to each other sharing brownies and
carrot cake.

They're the kind of people my brother says we're here
for. Affordable coffee and food, decent Wi-Fi, and no one
kicking you out if you sit too long.

By the end of my shift, I'm tired. I take off my apron as
I say goodbye to the baristas coming in for the night shift. I
grab my bag and phone, notebook tucked under my arm for
quick reviews during breaks.

I push open the side door, and stop.

He's there.

Jace leans against the lamppost outside the staff entrance,

one hand shoved into his jeans pocket, the other loose at his side.

"Hi," I say, a little awkwardly, throat tight. "Waiting for someone?"

"For you," he says simply, as if it explains everything.

I stare at him. "Why?"

"It's late," he says. "I'll walk you wherever you need to go. Or wait until you get a ride."

Something in me wants to argue, to say I can look after myself, to ask what kind of man waits outside a coffee shop for a girl he barely knows. Besides, I know how to handle myself. My father had made sure of that, since Luke and I were kids.

But the truth is, his presence doesn't feel wrong. It feels…protective. Maybe he's already claimed a right to be here, without me knowing.

"I don't need a ride," I tell him as we fall into step together. "I live just a few blocks away. Small apartment. Right next to my brother's. He makes sure I stay in school even with the business. I've got an exam tomorrow."

"You still study?" His gaze flicks to my face curiously.

"Of course I do. Accountancy, actually. I'm not letting Luke carry everything on his back." I hug the notebook tighter to my chest. "He's building something. And I want to be part of it, properly, as a partner in the business. What about you?"

He shrugs. "Computers. A little bit of this and that. Mostly contracts. Never got to finish college, but I get by. I live a few blocks out."

I sneak glances at him. The way the streetlamp hits the

sharp lines of his face. The scar half-hidden in the shadows. The way he carries himself—graceful yet quiet, every movement measured.

I can't even tell how old he is. He could easily be twenty-five or forty-five.

Jace doesn't say much as we make our way through the streets, but he doesn't need to. He walks close, his stride steady, like he's watching every shadow we pass.

He's not like anyone I know. He's not like anyone I should ever get close to.

And still, something in me wants to.

We stop at my gate. I should thank him, say goodnight, and go inside.

But instead, I look up at him and the words tumble out on their own. "You didn't have to walk me home."

"I did," he replies, the same way he did earlier.

I don't think.

I put a hand on his shoulder, to make him lean down. Then I rise on my toes and press my lips softly to his. Hesitant but quick, before my courage vanishes.

His breath catches, and I feel the smallest tension in him, as if he might pull me back in for more.

But he doesn't. He lets me have this one reckless choice.

I step away, cheeks hot, heart thundering. "Goodnight, Jace."

I slip inside the building, heart still racing, but I can't quite let it end. The kiss still burns on my lips. The warmth of him still clings to my skin.

So I walk to the small window by my desk and push the curtain aside.

He's still there.

Standing under the lamplight, shoulders squared like he belongs to the night itself. He doesn't move. Then, as if feeling my eyes on him, he looks up straight at my window, and catches me watching.

Heat floods my face and neck. But instead of hiding, I lift my hand and give him a wave.

For a moment, nothing. Then he raises his hand in return. Not playful, not shy—but steady, sure, a silent pact I know but don't understand.

It makes me smile anyway. My chest feels too full, like something new is blooming there, fragile but real.

I lower my hand, letting the curtain fall back into place.

On the street below, I know he's still standing there, still looking.

And I stand in my quiet little room, smiling into the shadows, already falling.

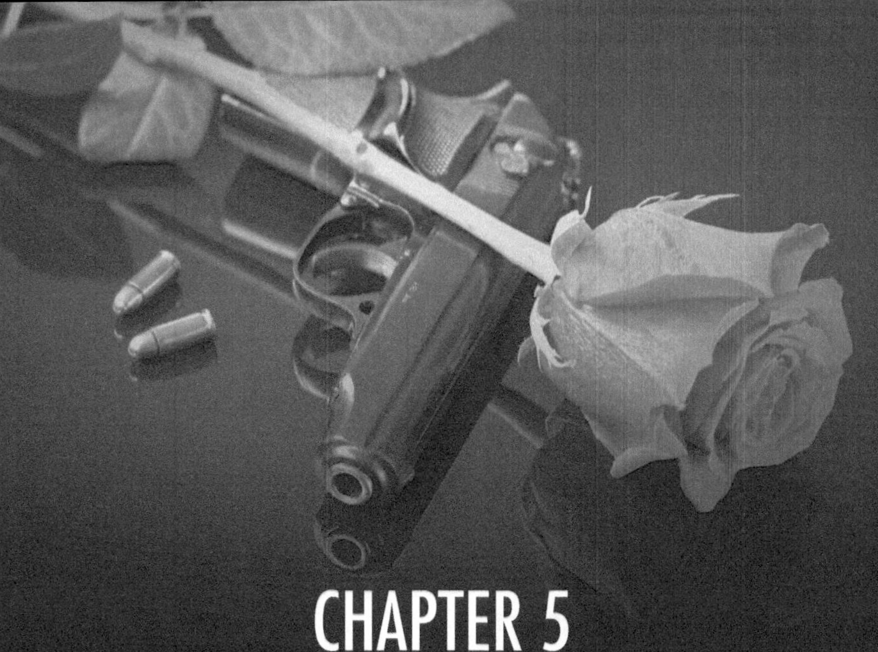

CHAPTER 5

I STAY UNTIL HER SHIFT ENDS.

I listen to the hum of the espresso machine, the sound of chairs scraping against tiles, and the voices of the students and call center kids as they drift out into the night. And still I sit, nursing a coffee gone cold, just to watch her.

Lara moves from table to table, clearing cups and plates. She hums under her breath, absentminded, something soft and tuneless.

She shouldn't be here, in this world where shadows like mine exist. She should belong to the light, where humming and laughter mean something.

Finally, she looks up and sees me still sitting there. Her eyes widen a little. "Jace. You're still here?"

I shrug. "Needed to see how you survived."

Her smile blooms instantly. The sight feels like a full round shot into my chest.

"The exams? Brutal. But I think I passed. Numbers never liked me, but I'm patient with them. Something's gonna give eventually, right?"

"Passing's enough." I lean forward, elbows on the table. "Your brother will be proud."

She tilts her head, studying me like she doesn't quite understand me. "You actually remembered I had exams."

"Of course I did."

Something flickers in her eyes. As if she's not used to people noticing, not like this. She tucks a strand of hair behind her ear, looking flustered, and murmurs, "Most people don't pay attention like that."

I try to smile. As best as I could. "I'm not most people."

She smiles back a little. "No. You're not."

She looks at me for a few more moments before she turns away to finish cleaning up. I watch her pull out her white handkerchief from her pocket and use it to pat away the beads of sweat clinging to her slender neck.

I have never seen something so innocent, yet so erotic. *Fuck it all.*

I should leave. I should end it here. But instead, I wait for her to finish up, then walk beside her into the night.

The streets are quiet, pools of yellow light stretching under the lampposts. A stray dog barks, a tricycle rattles past. When she looks at me, her eyes are tired, but soft, almost gentle.

"You don't have to keep walking me home, Jace. I'm used to this neighborhood."

"I know."

"Then why?"

"Because it's late." I glance at her, voice low. "And I'd rather it be me here than someone else."

She slows, just a fraction, as if the words caught her off guard. "You make it sound like the streets are dangerous."

"They are," I say simply.

She studies me, her eyes trying to see beneath the shadows I wear.

"Not when you're around," she replies.

Silence stretches between us. Every step toward her building feels like another step toward the edge of a cliff I can't stop myself from walking off.

At her gate, she stops, turning to me. The lamplight paints her in gold. .

She's nervous. I can see it in the way her fingers tighten on the straps of her bag, in the way her breath catches, but she doesn't look away.

"Jace…" Her voice is barely above a whisper. "You're… very different."

I don't ask what she means. I don't want to hear it.

And then she pulls me down by the shirt and kisses me.

It's soft and tentative at first, but it lingers, her hand brushing lightly against my chest. I feel her heart pounding as fast as mine. When she pulls back, her eyes are shining.

"You're a good man," she says softly.

The words cut through me, raw and merciless. I want to tell her the truth, that I'm anything but, that I'm the danger she doesn't see.

But my voice betrays me. "Don't say that."

"Why not?" she asks gently, almost smiling. "It's true. You look out for me. You don't even realize it, but you do."

Then she reaches up, her fingers lightly tracing over the scar on my cheek.

"You're very special," she says.

I can't breathe.

She doesn't know.

Her hand grazes mine as she lowers it and steps back toward her gate. "Goodnight, Jace."

And just like that, she's gone, door closing softly behind her, leaving me outside with my shadows and her words seared into my chest.

You're a good man. You're very special.

Just like the night before, I look up to see her standing by the window. She waves to me, a smile on her face.

I wave back.

Then I watch her draw the curtains. I don't move.

I stand there long after the lights in her apartment go dark.

And for the first time in years, I hate myself for the job I already agreed to.

❂

I tell myself not to come.

I tell myself to let her walk home alone tonight, to break the pattern before it becomes something I can't undo.

But I'm here anyway, across the street from where I can see her.

Inside the coffee shop, I see her moving, wiping down

a table as she talks to the men coming in for the new shift, stretching her arms like she's already half-asleep.

She's humming again. She doesn't know I hear her through glass, that I carry the sound with me into my dreams.

My chest aches. She waved at me. Smiled at me like I was hers to trust. And today, for hours, I thought about that smile. About her lips pressing to mine at the gate, soft and certain, calling me a good man, telling me I'm someone special.

I almost believed her.

Almost.

Then I remembered the file waiting in my room. Her photo clipped to the top. The promise I made to the woman who pays me to finish this.

And the truth—that nothing about me is good.

The side entrance door opens. Lara steps out, bag slung across her body. She pauses for a moment, glancing down the street.

She's looking for me. I see it in the way her eyes linger on the shadows, the faint crease of disappointment when she thinks I'm not there.

God. She wanted me here.

She starts walking. Her footsteps echo against the quiet pavement. I fall into step behind her, silent as I've been trained to be, my body a shadow among shadows.

Three blocks. Then two. My throat is dry.

I should let her go. I should vanish into the dark and forget her name.

I should let the job go.

But my feet move faster.

"Jace?" Her voice is uncertain when I finally step into the spill of the streetlight. She's not afraid. Not yet. She even smiles, faint and relieved. "I thought you weren't coming tonight."

My stomach twists. She doesn't know. She never saw the predator standing in the place of her protector.

I don't answer. I can't. I just reach into my pocket, feel the pouch of dust warm against my palm.

Her smile falters. "What's wrong?"

I step closer. Too close. The scent of coffee and her own cologne clings to her, now dangerously familiar.

"I'm sorry, Lara," I say. "Forgive me."

She opens her mouth to speak, but then I break the pouch, golden powder spilling into the night air.

She gasps, tries to push past me, but her body falters. "Jace…what are you—"

I catch her before she hits the ground. Her head falls against my chest, her lashes fluttering once before the darkness takes her.

I hold her tighter than I should. Too tight for someone who's only a job.

My heart slams against my ribs. She weighs nothing, but carrying her feels like bearing the whole world.

You're very special.

Her words echo in my skull.

You're a good man.

No. I'm not.

I lift her into my arms and disappear into the waiting shadows.

The water scalds my skin, but it isn't enough.

I turn the knob hotter, let it burn across my scar, down my chest, over the hands that carried her here. The sting is better than the cold inside me. Better than thinking about the way she said my name before the darkness closed around her.

Steam fills the bathroom, but it doesn't scrub me clean. The powder dust still clings to my conscience. The lie still rings in my ears.

You're very special. You're a good man.

I press my forehead to the tiles and breathe hard. If she knew who hired me, if she knew why, she'd spit at me, claw at me, even fight until she bled.

And yet she smiled at me. She kissed me. She waved from her window.

She believed in a man who never existed.

I twist the knobs off and step out, water trailing down my back, pooling on the tiles. I dry myself quickly, pull on a black shirt and joggers.

No mask now. No gun. Just me. The man in the shadows.

When I open the bathroom door, the room is hushed except for the low hum of the air-conditioner.

She's still asleep.

Lara lies curled on the bed, small beneath the weight of the hotel blanket, her long hair loose and spilled across the pillow. Her breathing is steady, lips parted slightly, face softened into something that feels too pure for the world she's been dragged into.

For a moment, I just stand there. Watching her. Listening to her breathe.

She looks peaceful.

I hate myself for knowing that peace will shatter in a few hours, when I take her to the rooftop. When the client arrives at dawn.

I drag a chair to the far side of the bed, lower myself onto it. My arms rest heavy on my knees, fingers knotting together as if they could hold me in place.

It should be easy. A job's a job. I've done worse.

But I can't stop staring at her. At the girl who called me good. At the girl who kissed me twice, and meant it.

Dawn is coming.

And I don't know if I have the strength to hand her over.

CHAPTER 6

THE FALL

S OMETHING THROBS AT THE BACK OF MY SKULL, DULL and insistent, pulling me up from the dark.

Flashes come back in pieces.

The street. A scarred face. A voice low in my ear.

The sudden blackness.

I open my eyes.

The room is half-dark, curtains drawn, the ceiling broken by restless shadows. A blanket covers me. The mattress beneath me is soft, molding to my body as though I belong here.

I don't.

My pulse spikes. I push the blanket aside, panic scraping raw against my throat. I'm still in my clothes. The white shirt and denim skirt are both intact, a little rumpled, still smelling faintly of coffee. Nothing has been taken from me but time

Where am I?

The street. The dust.

Jace.

A trap.

My breath hitches as I force myself upright. My body aches, nerves buzzing from whatever he used.

I can get through this.

I see something shift in the corner of the strange room. And I freeze.

He's there, standing at the foot of the bed.

Jace.

Even the shadows can't hide him. His dark eyes are unblinking, and the scar cuts a brutal line across his face. His hair falls loose, framing a jaw too sharp, too merciless.

"You." My voice is nothing but a hoarse whisper, but it fills the silence like a scream. "How could you do this? HOW?"

His eyes flicker. Surprise? Regret? I don't know.

My hand closes around the nearest thing I can reach. It's a glass lamp on the bedside table. I yank the plug free.

And before I can think, it's flying through the air.

He moves fast, but not fast enough. The lamp shatters against the wall beside him, shards spraying out like stars. One cuts across his right side. Blood blooms red against his forearm.

He curses low under his breath, clutching the wound.

I don't wait. I run out the nearest exit I can see.

I find myself on the balcony, wrapped in the heavy night air.

Wind slaps at me, whipping my hair across my face. My

chest heaves. I glance down. Endless city lights blur into dizzying streams of yellow and red.

It's too far, too high. If I jump, it's to my death.

Behind me, I hear footsteps.

He's coming.

I spin, throwing myself into a stance I've learned from Karate lessons our parents made me take since I was four. My body trembles, but I bare my teeth anyway.

"Get the fuck away from me, you bastard."

He doesn't answer. His eyes are unreadable, his steps deliberate, corralling me like prey.

I strike first. A kick to the midsection, enough to give me space to run past him. But he dodges it. His counter lands, palm to ribs, slamming the air from my lungs.

Pain cracks through me, and I stumble back.

The railing never catches me.

Only air. Only the plunge.

The world is a smear of black and neon and the howl of wind. I scream until my throat tears.

And then…

Impact. Not with the ground, but with him.

An arm locks around my waist, iron and heat. The rope bites above us, our single lifeline as the city spins below.

My scream dies into a gasp.

"Let me go," I choke out, but it's weak, almost pitiful.

"No." His voice is rough and harsh in my ear. "I can't."

I turn my head just enough to see his face.

The mask of shadows is gone. Only his eyes remain, burning and determined.

They're not the eyes of a monster. They're the eyes of a man bleeding.

A drop hits my cheek, warm and metallic.

Blood.

His blood. From the arm that holds the rope.

From the wound I gave him.

And still he holds.

We rise, inch by inch, until the railing meets us again. He shoves me over it. My legs shake as they find the solid surface of the balcony.

I want to run. But I don't.

He hauls himself after me, landing in a heap. His shirt is soaked, crimson smearing on his skin, his breath ragged.

We stare at each other, silence heavy as the night. He doesn't move. Doesn't reach for me. Just waits.

I could run. I should.

I kneel in front of him instead. "You're hurt."

His eyes flash in the shadows. "What are you doing?"

My handkerchief is already in my hands, trembling as I press it to his forearm. I knot it tight, clumsy but firm. Blood seeps through anyway. My throat aches. "That will help with the bleeding…for now."

When I look up, he's closer than I expected. Too close. Heat radiates off him, his gaze steady, as steady as the first time I looked into those eyes.

I should hate him. He kidnapped me. He dragged me into this nightmare. But my pulse won't calm, not with his heat seeping into me, not with his eyes dragging me under like tides I can't fight.

His face is inches from mine. His hand brushes my jaw,

his thumb grazing my skin like he has every right to. I should recoil. Instead, I shiver.

"Why?" I breathe.

"Because I can't stop," he says. "I can't let go."

Then his mouth claims mine.

The kiss is fire and steel, a clash of everything I should refuse and everything I can't resist. My hands curl into his shirt, pulling him closer, tasting blood and salt and him.

His tongue slides against mine, rough and starving, and I melt into him even as every nerve in me screams danger.

Everything else falls away—the city, the balcony, even the fear. My body betrays me completely, molding against his as though it's been waiting for this.

He drags me onto his lap, his thighs like iron beneath me, his chest hard and hot against mine. The cloth I tied around his forearm is already soaked, blood seeping warm through the fabric, but still his grip is unyielding. One hand digs in my hair, jerking my head back so he can take my mouth deeper, his tongue sliding hungrily against mine.

I moan into him. His other hand finds my hip, then my waist, then lower—gripping, squeezing, dragging me flush against him so I can feel every inch of his arousal pressing against the thin barrier of my skirt.

"Jace," I gasp against his lips, the word breaking.

"You feel that?" he growls, grinding me against him. "You do this to me, Lara. Every single time. That's why."

I shudder, my nails digging into his shoulders, my body rocking helplessly against his. Heat blooms everywhere, consuming and overwhelming.

I should fight. I should pull away. But instead I move

with him, straddling him more firmly, my thighs opening over his lap as if my body's already chosen for me.

His hand slips beneath the hem of my skirt, fingers brushing the bare skin of my thigh. I gasp and jolt, but his grip on my hair keeps me right where he wants me.

"Say it," he demands, his breath burning against my mouth. "Say you want this."

"I… I shouldn't…"

"Say it." His fingers skim higher, knuckles grazing the damp fabric of my panties.

A strangled whimper escapes me. "I want you."

He curses harshly, then his mouth is on mine again. His hand presses harder against me through the thin cotton, rubbing slow circles that make my whole body arch into him. My hips grind helplessly against his, chasing the friction, and his groan rumbles through both of us like thunder.

"Goddamn it, Lara," he rasps, biting my lip hard enough to sting. "You'll destroy me."

I'm already destroyed. My body trembles, my thighs shaking as he pushes me closer, closer, until the tension inside me snaps. Pleasure crashes through me, sharp and shattering, and I cry out against his mouth, my release spilling against his fingers.

He holds me through it, murmuring my name, his hand bruising on my hip. And even when the trembling subsides, he doesn't let go. He just pulls me tighter against him, grinding me against his hardness like he can't bear to stop.

I lean close, lips brushing his ear. "Let me give you this too."

His eyes widen, before he growls something low in his

throat. His grip loosens just enough for me to slide down, my hand trailing over his chest, his abdomen, until I reach the hardness straining in his pants.

He hisses through his teeth as I palm him firmly, feeling the weight of him hot and pulsing in my hand. His head falls back against the railing, his jaw clenched, a raw sound tearing out of him.

"Lara…"

I stroke him through the fabric, slow at first, then harder, faster, watching him come apart under me. He grabs my wrist like he wants to stop me, but he doesn't. He can't. He's panting now, hips jerking into my hand, his body trembling with need.

I draw closer, mounting him until my hips are just above his thighs. Enough for him to feel that whatever he's feeling, I'm feeling it too.

"Let go, Jace," I whisper into the night. "Let go."

He swears, a guttural sound, before crushing his mouth to mine again. His kiss is frantic, teeth and tongue and desperation, even as his release builds under my hand. When I finally reach inside his waistband and wrap my fingers around him, hot and rigid and slick with need, he shudders violently.

"Fuck…" he groans against my mouth, thrusting into my fist, every muscle in his body drawn tight. I stroke him harder and harder, faster and faster, my other hand tangled in his hair, until he breaks.

His release spills hot across my hand, across his skin, and he buries his face in my neck with a hoarse cry, clutching me like I'm the only thing keeping him alive.

For a moment, it feels like I am.

When his breathing finally slows, when the tremors ease, he cups my face in his hand. I can feel the rope burns on his palm. His eyes are molten, tortured, and tender all at once. He kisses me softly this time, a contrast so sharp it hurts.

And I know…we are not done.

Not even close.

I know what he wants. I know what *I* want.

For one wild, terrifying second, I want him to take me right here, on the balcony, under the stars with the city lights watching.

I'm still shaking when he kisses me again, his chest heaving. His hands are trembling as they find my cheeks, blood from his wound slick and sticky against my skin.

"I don't want to run," I say against his mouth.

"If I keep you," he rasps brokenly, fiercely, "I destroy you."

The words should terrify me. Instead, they break me open.

Because even as he says it, he goes hard beneath me, throbbing against the soaked cotton of my panties, his body trembling with the effort to hold back.

I can't let him.

I kiss the corner of his mouth, tasting salt and blood and pain.

And I say the words.

"Then destroy me."

CHAPTER 7

THE DAWN

SOMETHING INSIDE ME SNAPS.

I drag her against the cold concrete of the balcony, my hands rough, my body trembling with the kind of hunger I've buried since the moment I laid eyes on her.

The city is a blur below us, nothing but lights and noise. Here, it's only her. Her breath shudders into my mouth as I claim her lips, as if she's always been mine. I yank her skirt up, my hand pulling down the thin scrap of her soaked panties.

I stop for a moment. Not out of mercy, but because I feel her trembling, not just from fear.

I slide my fingers over her heat, testing and coaxing.

She's wet.

She's wet *for me*.

The realization nearly undoes me. So I do the only thing I could.

I lift her leg, nearly tearing her skirt in half, and bury my mouth in her. She tastes like cream, sweet and a little sticky, as my tongue lap at the juices from her earlier climax.

"Jace," she gasps, pulling at my hair with both hands, her hips jerking closer to my face.

I don't answer. Using my uninjured arm, I reach for her breasts under the cover of her shirt and bra, fingers stroking the nipples as my lips devour the soaking spot between her legs.

"I know, baby," I say against her thigh. "I know. You're ready for me."

"Jace," she says again, her knees bending over my shoulders as she writhes beneath me.

I slide up, covering her body with mine. It doesn't take long for me to lower the joggers, to free myself from the briefs completely. She moans as she pulls my shirt off, her teeth dragging across the bare skin of my chest, her hands digging into my arms, drawing more blood from the wound she'd given me.

And I'm above her, a breath away from making her completely mine.

"Tell me no, Lara," I rasp against her throat, my teeth scraping her skin. "I'll let you go. I promise."

One word could save her.

One word would save me.

"I won't," she says against my lips, then she drags her mouth to my scar, her tongue flicking out to trace it. "Never."

That single word breaks me. I push inside her, and the world explodes.

She gasps, her body so tight. Too tight.

My chest seizes when I realize.

She's untouched. Pure. I'm the first.

"Lara," I groan, my lips finding hers again. "God, you'll break me."

Her nails dig into my back, and I groan louder, half in agony, half in need. I can't stop. I move inside her, slow at first, then harder, deeper, claiming her in every way I know how.

She arches into me, tears glinting at the corners of her eyes, pain and pleasure tangled together.

"You'll destroy me, baby," I growl, kissing her hard, my hips driving her against the concrete until I feel it almost crack.

"Oh, god…Jace!" Her voice breaks on my name. "Don't stop. Please, don't stop—"

Her plea undoes whatever control I had left. I take her brutally, but my hand cradles her face, my mouth drinks every cry she makes. I move faster and faster, until I feel her clench around me, her scream muffled against my lips.

I spill into her with a ragged, broken cry, every drop of me claiming her. I clutch her as if letting go means death.

For one blistering moment, we're one. Flesh and soul and shadow.

When it ends, I collapse against her, our sweat and my blood between us.

Her scent clings to me. Her heartbeat thunders against my chest, wild and alive. And in that moment, I know the truth I've fought to deny since the beginning.

I love her.

God help me, I love her.

"I should never have touched you," I say, pressing my lips to her soaked hair.

Her hand cups my jaw, her eyes steady despite what I've made of her. "But you did. And I'll never regret it."

I kiss her once more. It's soft and reverent, because it's the last time I'll ever be allowed to. Then I pull away, the shadows closing back around me like a noose.

"Your bag's in the closet. Take my jacket if you want to."

She stares at me. "What are you talking about?"

I don't answer at first. Even as I stand before her bleeding, heart torn open, I help her back into her clothes. I put my arms around her waist and pull her up. I press my lips to her forehead, running my hand through her hair.

I know. I'll never get to touch her like this again.

"Run, Lara," I say softly. "This is the last mercy I have left."

She doesn't move.

"Jace…"

I turn away. "I promised I'll let you go."

Then I walk into the room and sit on the same chair at the foot of the bed.

She stumbles in after me, still wobbly on her feet. It doesn't take long for her to find her things. She slides my jacket on, the fabric swallowing her smaller frame.

She looks at me for the last time, reaching for the doorknob.

"I don't know what to say," she says, her voice small.

I smile at her. "You never had to say anything. Goodbye, Lara."

She doesn't answer.

In a breath, she's gone. Her hair loose, her skirt torn, my blood still drying on her skin.

I watch her from the balcony.

She reaches the street without incident, and mercifully manages to hail a taxi.

I should feel empty. Instead, I feel alive for the first time in years.

"Lara," I whisper into the night, her name torn out of me like prayer.

Like damnation.

I could chase her. I could take her back. I could burn the world down and keep her. I could wage war and win against impossible odds.

I could do it all for her.

But I don't.

Because if I love her at all, I have to let her go.

So I sink into the shadows again, bloodied and haunted, with nothing left but the taste of her on my lips and the fire she's branded into my heart.

And I wait for dawn to come.

RAIN CHECK

CHAPTER 1

STRONG WINDS

IT ALWAYS STARTS THE SAME.

The storm barrels in sudden and merciless, rattling the glass windows of the stores of the old commercial building. The wind howls, a large gust sending my umbrella to the side, bent and useless against the raging downpour.

Rain slaps against my skin as I make my way to the corner convenience store. I try to wrestle my umbrella back into place, but I'm already soaked through, shivering as thunder cracks overhead.

I realize the umbrella is broken. I've taped it back together in a few places before, but now the plastic has snapped clean through. Sighing, I toss it into an overflowing garbage can. I tell myself to buy a stronger one next time, but it also means skipping meals for a few days.

By the time I push through the glass doors of the store, I look half-drowned.

And he's there. As always.

I know him as Danny.

I heard a little old lady call him by the name once, while she was buying Vicks and some lozenges.

He's maybe thirty-something, lean and tall, bronze skin glistening where his sleeves are rolled up. He has tousled dark hair he never bothers taming, and eyes so dark they sometimes flash gray in the store's light. Tattoos run along his arms, half hidden by his shirt, dangerous and beautiful all at once.

He looks up from behind the counter, and something in me tightens out of instinct.

My heart pounds, nipples straining under my wet blouse, my body betraying just how much I ache for his attention. I tell myself I only duck into this shop for shelter as I await the mercy of the rideshare or taxi service to take me home.

But the truth is, I always find my way here because of him.

He grabs a towel from under the counter and holds it out without a word. Swallowing hard, I reach for it a little too quickly. When my fingers brush his, heat sparks through me, sharper than the storm.

"Thanks," I manage, hoping he couldn't hear my voice shaking.

This is the fourth time he has done this in the past two months, since I started seeking shelter at his store whenever it rains after my night classes at the College of Law.

"No problem." In contrast to mine, his voice is steady

and low-pitched. He slides a paper cup across the counter. "Coffee. On the house. With sugar, right?"

I nod and smile despite myself, wrapping both hands around the cup. The warmth seeps into my chilled fingers. "You don't even know my name, and now you're giving me free coffee?"

"Then maybe you should tell me," he says, leaning just slightly closer.

"Alya," I answer, more breathless than I mean to be.

"Alya." His lips quirk as he repeats the word. "I'm Danny. Pay me back when the sun comes out. Rain check."

I always come to the store at night, but I don't argue.

"Rain check," I echo instead. "Fine."

The heat of the coffee spreads through me, but it's nothing compared to the heat pooling low in my belly from the way he's looking at me. His gaze doesn't wander crudely, but it lingers heavily.

I bring the coffee to my lips, because I need the excuse not to drown in his black-gray eyes. My eyes almost flutter close at how good it tastes.

"Guess I owe you a lot already," I say.

"You don't," he murmurs. "The storms have been brutal lately. A place like this is meant for shelter, anyway. Besides, everyone in the city knows where Montalban Mini Mart is. Easier for your ride to find you."

I meet his eyes. He's looking straight at me, not even blinking. I square my shoulders, trying in vain to push down the blush creeping up my neck. "Still. You didn't have to."

He grabs a black plastic packet from under the counter.

He slides it toward me. When I touch it, I realize it's a pair of rubber slippers.

"You're going to wreck those shoes if you go home like that," he says softly.

This time, the blush sets my entire face on fire. "You don't have to do that."

"Only for regulars," he replies smoothly. "You've been in here enough times to qualify."

I bend my head down to hide my face, pretending to set my coffee and bag down on the counter. I slide my feet out of the soaked flats and ease them into the slippers.

"Feels like cheating," I say. "You're giving me too much."

When I look up, he hands me a small bottle of water, shrugging as he says, "Hydrate."

I stare at him, more surprised now than flustered. I want to ask him why he's doing all this. Why he notices my needs when no one else ever does.

Instead, I say, "You're…strangely prepared for rescuing half-drowned strangers."

He chuckles. "Not strangers anymore, Alya."

The sound almost undoes me, so I try to gather myself and do the only thing I could. The one thing he deserves.

I smile.

"No, Danny," I say. "Not strangers anymore."

He smiles right back, and my breath stops for a second.

"Good," he says. "Makes it easier when you show up again next time."

I incline my head, amused at his statement. "What makes you think I will?"

"Because the rain always comes back," he says simply. His gaze holds mine a beat too long. "And so do you."

I feel the flush in my face coming back full force. Just then, my phone pings, letting me know that the driver has reached the store.

I mutter *goodnight* and *thank you*, grabbing my bag, water bottle, and coffee as I go. I don't wait for him to answer.

Because he's right.

I'll be back. He knows it. I know too.

That's how it starts. Towels and coffee. Then he's added slippers and water.

His quiet care. My reckless need to be near him when the world around me is dark and drenched.

And now, the storm is raging louder inside me than outside.

CHAPTER 2

STORM SIGNAL

J UST LIKE ALWAYS, SHE APPEARS.

The moment the rain hits like a hammer against the glass, I know Alya will be at my door sooner than later.

She's gentle-looking and soft-spoken, but I can always see the steel flickering behind her eyes like lightning. She always looks put together even during the heaviest storms, dressed in bright-colored blouses and skirts.

Tonight, as she walks through the glass doors, her long dark hair hangs loose, dripping down her shoulders. Her light brown skin gleams wet under the fluorescent glow. Her umbrella hangs limp and loose from her right hand.

She shivers as she hobbles in, and I'm already reaching for the towel.

"Here," I say without preamble.

"Hi," she says as she takes it. "Me again. Thanks."

Her fingers brush mine, and it's enough to send a shudder straight through me, even though I'm comparatively warm and dry. I grab a paper cup and dispense the coffee from the machine the way she always takes it. As I wait for the cup to fill, I gesture toward the plastic stool I had set up by the counter.

"Sit. Dry off. You waiting for a ride?"

She nods, smiling faintly as she sets down her bag and umbrella on the floor, where I had also set up some hand-woven rugs to keep the surface dry and slippage-free.

"Yeah," she answers. "App says twenty to thirty minutes. I'll try not to flood your floor in the meantime. I like these mats you brought in, by the way. Very colorful."

I nod. "I got them from the market last Sunday. Scraps from tailoring shops, I believe. You seem to like colors, so I took a chance on the brightest-looking ones."

She blushes as she wraps the towel around her shoulders, then averts her eyes to take her coffee from the counter.

"Well, they're very pretty," she says. "I really like them."

"Glad you do," I answer.

She settles on the stool, still not looking at me.

Her voice is soft but curious when she finally speaks. "This store…it's been here a long time, hasn't it? Feels older than the others on this block. I remember it being around when I first came to the city."

"Yeah," I admit. "One of the oldest in town. My grandparents opened it, then my dad and mom took over eventually. It was supposed to go to my brother, Eddie. He… passed away a while back. So here I am."

Her expression shifts as she looks at me, sympathy

threading through her features, but it isn't pity. "I'm sorry. That must have been hard."

I nod. "It was. Still is. But the store's all I've got of my family, so I keep it running. Some of the employees have been with us for decades too."

She tilts her head, studying me. "So you're on your own then."

"I am." The words sit heavy on my tongue. "You?"

She takes a deep breath, as if weighing whether or not to say it. "Me too." Her eyes drop to her hands clutching the cup. "My father…he died years ago."

I don't speak, just wait. She glances at me, then looks away, words spilling like the rain outside.

"We had a farm in the province. He borrowed money from a rich businessman so I could go to college. Put the land up as collateral. He didn't really understand the documents. The businessman who wanted the land…they made sure of that. Well, there were typhoons that pretty much took all our harvests and my father missed more than a few payments. That was that. When they took everything—he couldn't live with it."

Her voice breaks. "My mother found him in the fields. He shot himself through the mouth with his *paltik*."

The breath I let out is ragged. "Alya…"

She shakes her head quickly. "My mother…she lasted a few months. Then a stroke. But I think she was already gone by then." She gives a shaky, humorless laugh. "I was lucky I had an aunt here in the city. She worked at a private school, got me a job in Admin when I finished college. She died two years ago."

Silence stretches between us, broken only by the hum of the refrigerators and the rain battering the glass.

Finally, I ask quietly, "And now?"

"Now it's just me." She lifts her chin, her voice steadier now. "I work days at the school. Go to law classes at night. I go to the college two blocks away. That's why I always find my way here."

"Law school," I echo. "That's no small thing."

Her smile is small, but fierce. "Someday I want to help people like my father. People who don't know the words on those papers. Who sign their lives away because no one explained it to them." Her eyes glisten, but her voice is hard and determined. "I won't let that happen again."

She's so damn brave it hurts. She's so damn *everything* it hurts.

"You're stronger than anyone I know," I tell her honestly.

Her phone pings, cutting through the moment. She glances down, then forces a smile. "My ride's here."

She stands up and hands me her empty cup and the towel back with a grateful nod. After gathering her bag and umbrella, she looks straight at me, eyes still bright with unshed tears.

"You've brought me good luck, you know," she says quietly. "I feel safe in your store. Every time I'm in here, I always manage to get a ride."

I walk her out into the storm, using one of the store's large umbrellas that we keep in our utility closet. The car idles at the curb, headlights slicing through the rain.

Alya pauses, then turns toward me, so close I can feel her heat through the chill.

Her eyes search mine, and before I can speak, she rises on her toes and kisses me.

It's not soft.

It's hungry.

Her lips part against mine, demanding and promising at the same time. A groan rips out of me before I can stop it, my free hand finding her waist, pulling her against me, every inch of her wet body molding to mine.

The kiss is lightning and thunder and everything I've been holding back for weeks since I first laid eyes on her.

She pulls back, breathless, lips swollen. Her smile trembles, but it's real. "Goodnight, Danny. Thanks for everything."

And then she's gone, slipping into the car, leaving me standing in the downpour with my umbrella, pulse hammering, the taste of her still burning in my mouth.

As I watch her disappear into the rain-drenched night, I already know.

I won't survive another storm without her.

CHAPTER 3

SECRET HEAT

IT ISN'T RAINING TONIGHT.

The air is still heavy with the day's heat, the sky streaked with thin clouds and the faintest shimmer of stars. It feels weird, walking to Danny's store without a storm pushing me toward it.

My heart beats fast, not from thunder this time, but from nerves. It's payday. I wanted to say thank you. And maybe…I just wanted to see him.

The plastic bag swings in my hand, warm with the weight of fried chicken and mixed meat noodles. I had to wait longer than expected at the restaurant nearby, and panic flutters in me as I hurry down the block.

What if he's already closed up?

What if I miss him?

But the store's lights glow steady. And when I push through the door, he's there.

Like always.

His head lifts, eyes catching mine. That dark, storm-gray gaze pins me.

The first thing he says makes me laugh, breathless with relief.

"It's not raining." His voice rumbles low, a smile forming on his lips as he speaks. "Are you okay?"

I nod, lifting the bag. "I brought dinner. To say thank you."

His smile curves wider, and something inside me falls—falls hard. Right then, I know I'm gone for him. Entirely.

"Dinner, huh?" He chuckles, a sound I want to trap and keep forever. "Guess I should get plates."

He moves to the tiny back office and returns with two mismatched plates and a pair of forks. He takes two cans of iced tea from the fridge and sets them up on the counter, next to where I have laid out the platters of chicken and noodles.

We sit and eat side by side, sharing food and warmth. Outside, the street is silent and still in the late evening. For a moment, it all feels almost ordinary.

"So," I venture, twirling noodles around my fork. "What about before the store? Before you took it over. Did you ever want to do something else?"

His jaw works, but the rest of him stills. "That's a loaded question."

I lean in, heart pounding. "I want to know, Danny. All of it. Whatever you'll tell me."

He sets down his fork, leans back, and breathes out slowly.

His voice is low as he speaks. "I was in prison. Got out a few years ago."

My chest tightens. "Prison? Why?"

His gaze locks on mine, his face expressionless. "Because I killed people. Four of them. For Eddie."

The room lurches, but I force myself to stay still.

"Your brother?" My voice cracks.

"Yeah." His voice roughens, cracking like thin glass under heavy weight. "Eddie was the golden one. Kind, steady, responsible. Took care of me when I was raising hell. Racing bikes, picking fights, wasting time. I was a joke to most people back then. Maybe I still am."

He pauses, dragging a hand down his face. "He was only two years older, but he was always there to pull me back. Keep me going in the right direction. He was my best friend."

I don't say anything when he stops speaking. Somehow, I know he's not done.

"One night, he was walking home after inventory," Danny continues. "Four guys jumped him. Took his money, his phone, his watch. And they stabbed him. Left him bleeding in the street like he was nothing. Knowing Eddie, he would have just given them what they wanted. He would not have put up a fight...unlike me."

A lump forms in my throat, hot and painful. "Oh, God..."

He goes on, his face unchanging. But his voice drops to something that sounds almost fragile.

"My parents were never the same after that. My dad even considered closing this store once, but his friends talked him out of it. And me?" His jaw flexes at the word. "I found them, Alya. Every last one of them. I killed them. One by one. Until there was no one left."

His eyes blaze with a pain that won't burn out, and I watch him, entranced.

"The police caught me after the fourth. I didn't fight it. My lawyer, one of Eddie's closest friends, got me a reduced sentence. I did my years. Got out on parole for good behavior."

He rolls up his sleeve, revealing the ink curling along his arm. "These? From my block. The guards called it Revenge Block. We're the guys who finished the jobs that other people couldn't. Not even our brave boys in blue."

"I was the *mayor* of the provincial jail for a while. It means I survived. You could say I even…thrived."

He looks at me closely, unblinking. "That's why I have the deepest respect for lawyers. If not for one, I could have just rotted away in prison. Because of Attorney Fabregas, I made it back out. Alone, but free for the most part."

I stare, unable to stop the flood of tears. My chest feels split wide open, raw and aching deeply.

"And your parents?" I manage to choke out.

He shakes his head slowly. "Gone before I got out. I came home to nothing but this store." His breath is ragged. "It's all I have left of my family. So I keep it alive. For Eddie. For my parents."

Danny reaches out, his fingers brushing my cheek with a tender hand. "And now…you're here with me." A wistful smile plays at the corners of his lips, the light slowly coming back into his eyes.

The fork slides from my hand, clattering against

porcelain. I push back my chair and cross the small space to him. My arms go around his shoulders, holding him tight. He stiffens at first, then exhales.

"I guess you can say I'm lucky, too," he says softly. "Right?"

His arms wrap me up, crushing me against him. His face presses into my neck, hot breath shuddering against my skin.

He smells like soap, rain, and something darker and more dangerous. It only makes me hold him tighter. His heart hammers against mine, and I feel every ounce of his own storm breaking open.

"You're not alone," I say, voice thick with tears. "I'm here."

His grip tightens like he'll never let me go. And then, slowly, he pulls back, just enough to look at me. His eyes burn right into mine, silvery and glittering. My breath catches at the sight.

Before I can speak, his mouth is on mine.

It's rough and desperate, his lips devouring me like he's been starving for years. A cry escapes me, muffled against his mouth as his hands slide lower, gripping my hips, dragging me onto his lap.

I straddle him without thought, the stool creaking under us as his hands cup my butt, squeezing hard enough to make me gasp. Heat sears through me, pooling low and hot in my stomach, my nipples hardening under my blouse as he presses me closer to him.

"Danny," I whisper against his lips, shuddering as his tongue sweeps into my mouth.

He groans raggedly, and grinds me down against the hard length straining through his jeans.

"You drive me crazy," he rasps. "Every damn time."

I clutch his shoulders, dizzy with need, and kiss him back like I'll never get another chance. Tears and hunger blur together, heartbreak turning into fire, into something I can't fight anymore.

I don't ever want to.

He groans low in his chest, and suddenly his hands are on my waist. He lifts and sets me down on the counter with a roughness that makes me squeal in surprise. The plates rattle, one tips over and clatters to the floor, but neither of us cares.

He reaches beneath my blouse, palms tracing their way over the bare skin of my stomach until his hands cup my breasts under my bra, his thumbs rubbing the nipples in slow circles, making me writhe against him.

"Alya." My name leaves him hoarsely. "Tell me to stop. Tell me and I'll stop."

My hands cup his face, trembling but certain. "Don't stop."

"*Fuck*," he says raggedly. "I'm starving. I'm starving for you."

His hands go lower, down my waist, then moves along my thighs, pushing them open. Then his mouth is on mine again, his hands dragging my skirt higher, higher, until I'm trembling with the exposure, the danger, the need. He kisses down my jaw, my throat, the frantic rise of my chest. Each brush of his lips breaks me open, until I'm shaking, until I can't think.

"Danny," I whisper as he slides off my panties.

"It's okay," he answers. "I've got you. I've always got you."

Then his hand takes over. He caresses and rubs, fingers stroking and moving in and out of me, gently at first, then with more urgency. Under his touch, I feel my body come alive, warm and wet and wanting.

When his head lowers further, his eyes meet mine, dark and burning, asking without words. My answer is in the way I arch toward him, in the way my fingers tangle in his hair.

And then his mouth claims me.

The shock of it rips a cry from my throat, sharp and unrestrained, echoing throughout the store. My body jolts, my knees clamping instinctively around his shoulders, but his grip is firm, holding me wide for him. The first stroke of his tongue is scorching, every nerve in me coming alive.

"Danny—" My voice breaks, begging for more as I lift my hips toward the release that his tongue and lips are promising.

He moans against me, the sound vibrating through every inch of my body, and it undoes me. I tip my head back, clutching fistfuls of his hair, legs jerking helplessly as he devours me. Heat floods in my belly, building fast, too fast, until I'm whimpering his name.

"You taste like heaven," he rasps against me. "You were made for me, Alya. My own heaven."

And then I'm gone, breaking against his mouth, sobbing and gasping for air, every ounce of me ripping into pieces under him. He holds me through it, his hands strong on my thighs, his lips and tongue relentless as he finishes me off, until I collapse back on the counter.

When he finally lifts his head, his lips are slick, his eyes blazing and tender all at once. He kisses my inner thigh, then my knee, then he finally rises.

I'm still shaking when his chin lands above my head, his lips brushing against my hair. His arms cage me on the counter, his breath hot against my cheek, his chest rising and falling.

He's breathing as hard as I am, voice raw when he mutters, "I've been starving, Alya. And I'll never get enough of you."

And I know I'm lost.

I know I am completely, irrevocably his.

That's when it hits me.

He hasn't had anything. He gave me everything, and he's still burning.

His hunger presses against me where our bodies touch.

Now I want to feed him, to take care of him, the same way he just took care of me.

Before I lose my nerve, I slide down from the counter, using his shoulders to pull myself down. My knees sink into the rugs on the floor.

He freezes above me, his eyes going wide. "Alya, you don't have to—"

"I want to," I cut him off, my voice shaky but certain. My hands rest on his thighs, feeling the heat of him through denim. My heart pounds so hard I can barely breathe. "I've never…done this before. But I want to. For you."

He groans, rubbing his hands over his face like he's fighting himself. "Christ. You're gonna kill me."

I swallow hard, fingers fumbling as I push him toward the counter. I feel clumsy and terrified, but determined. His hands hover near my face, as if he's afraid to touch me and afraid to let me go at the same time. When I unzip him and pull down his jeans and briefs, he shudders like the world just cracked open.

Then I see the length of him, rock-hard and red and starving for me. My hands close around him, then I take him into my mouth.

His head tips back, a broken sound ripping from his chest. "Oh, God, Alya…"

Every reaction of his—every gasp, every ragged moan, every jerk of his hips—ignites me. I've never felt power like this, never felt someone come undone because of me. He digs his hands in the counter behind him, muscles locked, body shaking.

I keep going, using my hands, my tongue, my lips, finding a rhythm, my nervousness fading under the rawness of his need. The way he curses under his breath, the way my name falls from his lips—it all makes me braver.

"You have no idea," he gasps out, his hands moving to my hair and his hips starting to thrust in time with my mouth, "what you're doing to me."

The sound of his voice, thick with devastation and desire, makes me feel light-headed. My hands clutch tighter, my whole body humming with heat as I give him everything I can.

And when he finally breaks, when his control shatters and he groans my name like it's the only word he knows, I feel it through every inch of me.

His release is raw, almost violent, but his hands cup my face after, tender and trembling, pulling me up into his arms.

He kisses me almost reverently. "You…you're everything. I don't deserve you, but God help me, I'll never let you go."

I'm breathless and shaking, lips swollen and heart burning, and all I can think is…

I don't want him to.

CHAPTER 4

SKY FALLING

THE STORM HASN'T STOPPED SINCE SUNDOWN.

Rain pours relentlessly over the city, rivers crawling down the street, floodwater creeping past the gutters. I ask Willie, the young stockboy who had taken over from his father, to drop off the old cashier, Carmen, and go on straight home. I tell them we might not even open the store in the morning.

They fuss about me staying and tell me to go home, too, but I wave them off. This isn't the first time I've ridden out a storm alone.

But tonight isn't like every other night.

It's past seven. My eyes keep flicking to the clock, then the door. Alya's classes don't finish until nine, but already my chest is tight, almost restless.

Two nights ago, she brought me dinner and nearly broke me open on the counter with her warmth, her kiss, her touch.

With all of her.

The way she held me after, as if I was worth saving.

I didn't ask for more. I just made sure she got into a car safely before I locked up. But the taste and the feel of her has been burning in me since.

I wait. I pace. The minutes crawl, and the storm only grows worse.

By fifteen past nine, my hands dig into the counter, the same place where I had lifted and stripped and tasted her only nights ago.

But still no Alya.

By half past nine, my pulse is thundering louder than the rain. Rage and fear coil together until I can't sit still another second.

Then the power flickers—and dies.

The store sinks into blackness, thunder splitting the sky.

"Fuck this."

I grab my phone, its glow cutting a pale circle in the dark. I don't hesitate anymore. I lock up fast, splash into the street, the water cold and rising around my boots.

The city is empty. Shuttered shops, no cars, no people. Just storm and silence. I run hard, water slapping up to my calves, until I reach the alley down the block. The garage door groans as I haul it open. My bike waits in the shadows, untouched for months.

"C'mon, baby," I mutter, swinging my leg over. The engine coughs, then roars, vibrating through me. I gun the throttle, spray kicking up as I swerve into the drowned city.

The streets are blacked out, water up to the hubs, but the machine growls steady beneath me.

I ride toward the college, headlights slicing through thick sheets of rain. Every block feels endless. My chest aches with the thought of her out there alone, soaked and cold. By the time I see the faint silhouette of the waiting shed in front of the campus, my heart nearly rips through my ribs.

There she is.

Alya is huddled under the crooked roof, rain tearing at her broken umbrella, water rushing ankle-deep around her. Her hair is plastered to her face, her bag clutched to her chest, but she's still standing.

Still fighting.

The second she sees me, her lips curve in the smallest, fiercest smile.

"I'm glad you came." Her voice is shaky but strong. "The water was too deep to get through to your shop. And no drivers would take me. Said the flood was too high."

I kill the engine, splashing to a stop, water soaking through my clothes.

"It's okay," I rasp, swinging off the bike. "This motorcycle's tough. It can take a little water."

But I don't give her the chance to say more. I reach her, grab her, drag her against me with a force that's half desperation, half relief. My arms wrap her up tightly.

She gasps against my chest. "Danny, I—"

I cut her off with my mouth. The kiss is wild, rain-slick, teeth and tongue and heat. She tastes like storm and survival, and I drink her down. Her hands clutch at my shirt, holding me just as hard, answering every ounce of my hunger with her own.

When I manage to tear myself away to speak, I don't let her go.

"You're not alone anymore. You hear me? You've got me. Always."

Her eyes shine in the pale light, wet from more than the rain. She nods once, trembling, and pulls me down into another kiss.

This time, it feels like a promise in the middle of the drowned streets.

And I promise myself I'll burn the whole world before I let her stand alone again.

"Don't leave me alone," Alya whispers against my lips, her breath trembling. "Please, Danny. Don't ever leave me alone."

My hands cup her face, thumbs brushing away the rain streaming down her cheeks.

"I won't," I say. "I promise I won't."

"Maybe…this is where I belong," she says, eyes wide as she looks at me. "With you. That's why I keep coming back to the store whenever there's a storm. Because you're the only person I've ever met who makes me feel like I could never be hurt, even when the world is angry."

The confession cracks something inside me. She's shaking, but she keeps talking, almost like a lost girl finding her way home in the dark.

"The first time I saw you," she says, "you got me the coffee I wanted. And you refused my payment. You said, 'Rain check, miss.'" Her lip trembles. "You always said it to me, but to me it meant…" Her voice trails off, then she takes a deep breath and continues. "It meant you would always welcome me back, even at my worst. That's why I just kept coming back to you, Danny. I didn't know where else to go."

I pull her against me, arms locking around her small, soaked frame, pressing her head to my chest. My throat is tight, my own eyes stinging. "Alya…"

She buries her face against me, words muffled. "You're the only place I've ever felt safe."

I lower my mouth to her ear. "Then let me take you home. Let me love you the way I've always wanted to."

She jerks back. "What?"

"I love you." My voice is hoarse but steady. "I've loved you from the first storm you walked into."

Her head shakes wildly, rain flying. "How can you say that? I'm nobody. I can't even afford an umbrella half the time. I don't have anything to give you, Danny."

I catch her chin, make her look at me. "No, Alya. I love you because *you* are everything. You're brave, strong, relentless. You walk through storms and still show up. You survived everything, and you're still here." My thumb strokes her cheek, then I trace its path with my lips. "And you're the most amazing and beautiful woman I've ever laid eyes on. You're my everything, even if you think otherwise. I guess I'll just spend the rest of my life trying to convince you."

Something in her breaks open at my words. She lets out a sob, then leaps up, wrapping her arms around my neck, clinging to me like she'll drown if she lets go. I hold her tight, burying my face in her wet hair.

"Take me home," she chokes out. "Get me out of here."

I scoop her up against me, her legs locking around my waist, and carry her to the bike. The engine roars back to life under us, headlights slicing through the flood as we surge into the rising water together.

For the first time in years, I don't feel alone.

CHAPTER 5

SHADOW STORY

THE RAIN LASHES AGAINST MY FACE AS DANNY DRIVES us through the flooded streets, the motorcycle cutting through dark water.

My arms are wrapped tight around his waist, cheek pressed to his back. Every muscle in him hums with focus, but I can feel the way he eases closer whenever we hit a deeper patch. His body feels like a shield against the storm.

We reach the store's block, an older part of the city where buildings rise narrow and tall. He doesn't stop at the corner but keeps going instead, driving into a wide alley lined with steel gates, their courtyards inside half-drowned. He pulls into one, the engine rumbling low before he cuts it off. My ears ring with silence, except for the endless rain.

"This way," he says.

His hand finds mine and he leads me off the bike,

through the arch of the courtyard, toward a worn staircase that creaks under our steps. The power's still out, the building sunk in darkness, but Danny lifts his phone, the small torch casting a pale halo over his face.

Shadows carve along his cheekbones, catching in the wet strands of his hair, and he looks younger somehow. Almost shy.

"This is the way things used to be done here," he says softly, his voice carrying in the stillness. "People lived above or beside their shops. My parents did."

The admission makes my heart tighten. He's always so solid, so strong and infallible, but right now, in the flickering light, I see the boy he once was, still living with ghosts.

The lock of the heavy wooden door clicks open, and he ushers me inside. The apartment smells faintly of wood and rain.

Danny sets his phone on a table and switches on two emergency lamps. The glow from them is warm enough, pushing back the dark.

The apartment is simple and clean, but old. Around me are cabinets with chipped handles, sofas with threadbare arms, and low tables with scratches. The floor is covered with patterned linoleum.

On the wall, framed photographs hang in careful lines. A couple, most likely his parents, smiling, their arms around each other. A boy who looks similar to Danny but with neater hair and calmer eyes, holding a trophy, his grin easy and kind.

Danny's voice is low as he follows my gaze. "That's Eddie. He always kept this place alive, even when I was being a pain in everyone's ass. My parents…they left it just the way it was.

Can't imagine what it must have been like for them. Eddie gone. Then I was put away." He swallows, then looks back at me. "When I got out, I came back here. It still felt like home, even if they weren't around anymore."

He picks up one of the portable lamps, gesturing down the narrow hall with his free hand. "The other rooms are empty. No one's lived in them since. Just me."

I follow him as he leads the way. He stops at a doorway at the end of the corridor.

"This is mine." He runs a hand through his wet hair and tries for a smile as he turns the knob and pushes the door open. "You can stay here as long as you want. No strings attached. Just…home."

The word echoes in me, deeper than I expect.

Home.

Light spills on a small space, with wooden floors and a surprisingly neat bed with white sheets. The walls are bare, lined on one side with worn cabinets. A few books are piled next to a small lamp on the nightstand.

It isn't grand, but it feels safe.

It feels real.

Danny clears his throat, almost awkward now, as he hands over the emergency lamp. Our fingers brush lightly, but he pulls back.

"I'll try to find something to eat. Might be cold, but it's better than nothing. I've got some clothes in the cabinet if you want to change."

He hesitates at the door, his hand on the frame. In the lamplight, his eyes are softer than I've ever seen them, uncertain. He looks like he's standing at the edge of something he never thought he'd share.

"Get comfortable," he says quietly. "I'll be right outside."

The door shuts behind him, leaving me in the dim glow, my heart pounding.

Then it hits me with the force of the storm outside.

This man, this room, this night…it's all a revelation.

For the first time in years, I feel like I might finally belong somewhere.

The light never comes back on.

The storm presses against the windows, heavy and loud, the rain a constant roar. I move carefully by the glow of the emergency lamp Danny left me.

I peel off my wet clothes, shivering as I pour water from the bathroom bucket over myself. It's cold, but it clears the storm from my skin. I wash off the taste of fear, the weight of the street.

I towel off, then rummage through his cabinet until I find a pair of old shorts and a plain shirt that hang loose on me but still smell faintly of him.

When I open the door, the hall is aglow with lamplight. Not the chargeable battery lamps from earlier, but real kerosene lamps, their flames flickering gold.

Danny glances up from the table. He's changed, too, into a fresh white shirt and loose dark shorts. His hair is damp, curling at the ends.

"These used to belong to my grandparents," he says,

almost shyly, tilting his head toward the lamps on the table. "Everyone had something like this in the old days, I guess."

On the six-seat dining table between us, there are bottles of water and two steaming cups of noodles.

He nods toward a chair. "Not much of a feast, but it's hot. I've got some more boiled water if you want to have coffee later."

We eat in silence at first, rain filling the spaces between our words. Then small talk slips in. We talk about harmless things. The taste of the broth. The memory of storms past and how the building and the store survived then.

He doesn't touch me. Not once.

It surprises me. After everything, after what happened on the counter, I thought…

But maybe he's holding back. Maybe he doesn't want to break whatever this fragile, impossible thing between us is.

When we finish, he gathers the cups and bottles, moving to clean up.

I watch him in the lamplight. Broad shoulders, wet hair, careful hands, the quiet patience in him…and I can't take it anymore.

I cross the room and press myself against his back, my arms sliding around his waist. He freezes, then slowly turns, setting the dishes aside.

He bends to kiss my forehead, his lips lingering there. "You should rest," he murmurs. "Do you need paracetamol? You've been through a lot tonight."

I shake my head. "No."

He exhales, half a laugh, half in what seems to be

disbelief. "I still can't believe you're here. That you're with me and…" His voice falters.

I nod, cutting him off. "Put it away, Danny. All of it. The worry. The doubt. Because yes. I'm here. We're both here. We're home. And I belong with you."

And I see it in his eyes.

The control he's been gripping slips loose. His hands are suddenly on my face, his mouth crashing to mine with a hunger that steals my breath.

The kiss is wild and desperate. I gasp as his hands slide down, gripping my hips, my ass, hauling me up against him. His body is hard and unyielding, his groan tearing through the quiet.

We stumble, then fall together onto the floor, the linoleum cold under my back, his weight pressing me down. His hands are everywhere—palming, clutching, greedy— as he tears my borrowed shirt up over my head and drags my shorts down my legs, stripping me bare in the flickering lamplight.

I arch, helpless beneath him, naked and trembling. His mouth breaks from mine only to trail down my throat, my chest, lower still, until his breath sears hot against the most fragile part of me.

"Danny…" My voice is a soft, pleading cry.

His eyes lift, molten gray in the golden glow.

"Mine," he growls. "You're mine, Alya."

Then he bends and devours me, and the storm outside has nothing on the storm that breaks inside me.

Danny's mouth pulls me apart until I'm shaking, until

every breath is a whimper. My body still hums when I reach for him, tugging at his shirt.

"Let me," I whisper, hands clumsy, but more determined than ever.

His eyes darken, breath catching as I peel his shirt away. My palms skim his chest, his skin hot and alive under my fingertips, muscles rippling like coiled ropes of strength. He's beautiful, ink curling down his arms and around his torso, scars etched faintly across his skin.

He's breathtakingly real, a man made of storms and survival.

I touch lower and lower, tentatively, and he groans, catching my wrist but not pushing me away. His restraint shakes through him, but he lets me explore, lets me learn the shape of him with my hands.

"Alya," he rasps. "You don't—"

"Let me," I cut him off. "I want this."

My voice almost falters, but the truth in it steadies me as I pull down his shorts and briefs.

His control breaks. He leans down, kissing me hard, then softer, trailing over my cheek, my throat, my collarbone, his hands cupping my breasts, thumbs brushing over my hard nipples until I arch helplessly beneath him. His mouth follows, hot and hungry, worshipping me in ways that leave me gasping.

He lingers between my thighs, caressing and teasing and licking, until I'm undone again, pleading for him without words.

Then he stills.

Rain hammers the roof, thunder rolls, but his whisper cuts through everything.

"I love you, Alya."

My breath catches. "Danny, I—"

"I love you," he says again, fiercer this time. To my ears, it sounds like the only truth he's ever known. "From the first time I saw you walk into my store and my life. From the first rain check. Always."

Tears sting my eyes, mingling with sweat. I wrap my legs around him, pulling him closer, needing him. Needing this.

"Then take me," I breathe. "Because I love you too."

His mouth claims mine as he gently lowers himself over me. His hands cradle my face and stroke my hair as he slowly enters me. He lets me adjust, waiting patiently with kisses and soft, soothing whispers.

I clutch him tight as I feel him inside me, my body molding to his, then I begin to move. My hips meet his and he groans and curses, then he matches my rhythm with thrusts that become harder, faster, and more desperate.

The world narrows to the heat of his skin, the press of his chest, the worship in his eyes, the pleasure that sears throughout my body as he pounds into me.

His mouth finds my breasts, his name falls from my lips, and I give myself to him completely, wrapped around him as the night swallows us whole.

And in the darkness, in his arms, I finally understand what it means to be home.

CHAPTER 6

STOLEN KISS

THE STORM OUTSIDE DOESN'T LET UP, BUT INSIDE, I can't get enough of her.

Alya is under me, around me, trembling and fierce, and every time she gasps my name it's like a match striking inside my chest. I'm starving, and I know it shows in the way I kiss her, the way I can't stop touching her, the way I keep pulling her back when she tries to breathe.

We burn through the night, moving like the storm wind itself is chasing us. The linoleum floor becomes too small, so I lift her and set her on the table where we ate not an hour ago. The bowls and bottles scatter to the floor, and she laughs breathlessly before I swallow the sound with my mouth.

Her laughter, her tears, her cries—I take them all, because they're mine now, every one.

When the table groans, I carry her again, settling her

on the sofa, sinking into the worn cushions with her spread across me, my hands holding her by the ankles as I take her more slowly, more deeply.

And when we're done that way, I ask her to get on top of me.

The flickering lamplight paints her skin gold, and I can't stop staring at her. Alya's hair is loose and wild around her, her eyes still heavy with need, her lips swollen, but she rides me like a goddess as I squeeze her breasts, surprisingly full for someone as petite as her. She leans down to kiss me, and I think I could die like this, drowning in her.

But even the sofa can't contain us. I press her gently against the wall, her body arching into mine, her nails digging into my back, and I whisper against her ear, "You're everything. Do you know that? You're everything."

She whispers it back, and the sound tears me apart. I pound into her harder, mouth lowering to take her nipple, and she cries out, rubbing up and down, taking every inch of pleasure I am giving her.

By the time I carry her into my room, we're both shaking, but I still want more. I set her down on my bed—the bed I've slept in alone for years, the bed my parents kept waiting for me while I was locked away—and tonight, it finally feels alive.

She looks at me, wide-eyed, uncertain but brave, as I bend her on all fours at the edge.

I know I have to show her. Not just what it means to be touched, but what it means to be loved completely.

Then I take her from behind, my hands going around to cup her breasts, my lips and teeth nipping at the back of her neck.

I guide her, teach her how to move with me, how to let go of the fear, how to give in to the hunger that's been between us since the first storm.

Every time she hesitates, I hold her. Every time she falters, I kiss her. And when she grows bolder, when she learns the rhythm of us, I almost lose myself in the wonder of it.

We make love and fall together through the night, over and over, until the storm outside fades into the gray hush of dawn, until she collapses on top of me, her body tangled with mine, hair damp against my chest, breath warm on my skin. I stroke her back, slowly and lightly, as the sun begins to rise behind the curtains.

For the first time in years, I don't feel restless. I don't feel haunted. I feel…whole. Because Alya is in my arms, and she's never leaving.

I kiss the crown of her head, whispering into her hair as sleep finally drags me under.

"I love you. Always."

And she stirs against me, murmuring her answer, "I love you too."

The first thing I notice is the quiet.

No pounding rain, no cracking thunder, no rushing water. Just the soft hum of a city wrung out by a storm.

Then I see her next to me.

Alya's curled into me, hair spread like ink across the pillow, her cheek pressed against my chest.

My arm is numb beneath her but I don't dare move. Not yet. I just watch. The rise and fall of her breath. The way she clutches the blanket like she's afraid it will slip away.

I've always woken up alone. In prison. In this apartment. In silence. But now…now there's someone beside me. Someone warm. Someone real.

Someone I love.

Her lashes flutter, and then her eyes blink open, soft and sleepy, finding mine. For a second, we just stare at each shyly, like two kids caught doing something forbidden.

Then she gives me the smallest smile, and I'm done for.

"Good morning," she whispers.

"Good morning," I manage, my voice rough.

A sharp ping breaks the spell. She leans across me to grab her phone from the nightstand, the blanket slipping, her bare breast brushing my shoulder. I bite back a groan. She scans the screen, then laughs softly.

"School's closed. Flood's too bad in the city to go anywhere." She sets the phone down, looking back at me, eyes gleaming.

I raise a brow, smirking. "Well. Looks like you're stuck with me."

She giggles, light and unguarded. And before I can blink, she swings a leg over, straddling me. My breath leaves me in a rush.

"Alya…"

Her lips brush mine teasingly, then her tongue flicks out to trace my lower lip. "Rain check?"

Heat slams through me, shattering any control I thought

I still had. I grip her hips, my head falling back against the pillow with a helpless laugh. "Hell, no."

She shifts her weight just enough to make me groan, her hair falling like a curtain around us. The blanket slides off her body, and her skin feels like warm silk against mine. My body responds before I can think, hard and aching beneath her.

Her smile tilts wickedly. She rocks once, very slowly, and I choke out a sound I haven't made in forever.

"You're a greedy goddess," I rasp, clutching her thighs, staring up at her like she's a vision I don't deserve.

Her eyes glimmer with mischief and fire. "Why else do you think I keep coming to you? Every single time?" She grinds again, teasing and tormenting. "I know what I want."

A curse breaks from my throat. My hands grip her harder, sliding up her waist, her back, her breasts, desperate not to lose my mind.

"You're killing me," I groan.

"No," she whispers as she leans down, her mouth ghosting over mine. "I'm keeping you alive."

And she's right. Every move from her body, every taunt in her voice, every kiss she steals…it's life itself.

A life we might just live in love, through whatever storms may come.

I surge up, sealing my mouth to hers, tasting her laugh, her moan—all of her. The blanket tangles, the room spins, and I know I'll never get enough.

I'm hers. Always.

No rain checks.

Not ever.

SUNSETS IN SEPTEMBER

CHAPTER 1

ANOTHER YEAR

Every September, I return.

The pier is the same as it was the day he first brought me here.

The wooden planks are still weathered by salt, while sea spray still mists the air. I can still hear fishermen's laughter echoing down the rails.

My fiancé used to say this place feels like forever.

But forever never came.

He died in a highway accident three years ago.

But I still come on his birthday and stay for a few days. Every day I'm here, I sit at the edge of the pier with a paper cup of coffee, watch the sun burn the sea gold, and pretend he's beside me.

Only this year, I'm not alone.

There's a man standing at the rail, hands in his pockets,

shoulders broad under a navy button-down. His presence is quiet but steady. He glances at me once—dark eyes, sharp looking but tired—and nods.

I nod back.

That's all. But it's enough to unsettle the rhythm of my ritual.

The next evening, he's there again.

"Hi," he says, voice deep and even.

"Hi."

We stand side by side, not quite close but not far. He smells faintly of something cool and smoky.

On the third evening, he says, "You come here often?"

"Every September," I admit. "This is my third."

His lips twitch, like he understands more than I said. "My first time this year."

There's silence. The sea roars before us. I want to ask him why, but something in his face, one deeply etched with lines of time and loss, stops me.

We don't trade stories.

Just quiet nods, shared sunsets, and the small comfort of knowing someone else carries ghosts too.

CHAPTER 2

ANOTHER ENDING

THE PIER IS CROWDED TONIGHT.

Too crowded.

Vendors line the planks shoulder to shoulder, grills smoking, oil popping, the air thick with salt and roasted corn. Children dart between legs, barefoot and laughing, balloons tugging against their strings as if they want to escape. Couples lean into each other, whispering secrets and laughing. Families take photos in front of the water as if the sea is something that can be owned and framed.

I don't come on nights like this.

But it's her last night.

I just know it is, even before she checks her watch, or before her shoulders sag just slightly. She gets to her feet and takes that last, lingering look at the horizon like she's saying goodbye without wanting to admit it.

Patterns are my job.

People think grief is chaotic, but it really isn't. It's precise. Almost ritualized. Predictable in the way pain always is.

She waits for the sky to turn.

Orange first, then gold. Finally, that deep, aching purple that settles into your bones if you stare too long. The color my wife used to chase with her phone camera, always a second too late. The color this woman has been waiting for every night since I first saw her sitting alone with a paper cup of coffee, pretending she wasn't.

I watch her as she turns. She's statuesque and graceful, long dark hair streaming behind her back as she moves slowly through the crowd. Her almond-shaped eyes gaze ahead, but they don't really take in anything.

There's a difference between looking and seeing. One I know all too well.

When she finally heads toward the narrow road back to town, I hesitate.

I've followed her every night this week. Always at a distance. Always telling myself it's instinct, not interest. Professional habit. The world doesn't stop being dangerous just because you're off duty.

So I follow her.

The crowd thins the farther she walks from the pier lights. Shadows stretch longer. I spot the man before she does.

He stands too close, too intently, gaze locked on her bag instead of the sea.

My pace changes.

He grabs her strap.

She stumbles and shouts, panic flaring.

Something old and violent coils in my chest.

I move.

Training takes over. The noise drops away. I grab his wrist, twisting hard. I feel the give, the yelp. Her bag comes free.

I shove him off balance, just enough. He curses, scrambles, and runs into the dark.

I let him go. He isn't worth the paperwork.

She's shaking when I turn back, clutching her bag like it's a lifeline, eyes wide, breath coming too fast.

"Are you okay?" I ask, forcing my voice steady.

"Yes," she says. "Yes. I think so."

I don't realize how tight my shoulders are until I breathe out. I reach for my badge, flashing it briefly, automatically, for her to see.

"I'm a cop," I say quietly. "Senior Inspector Brian Medina."

Understanding dawns in her eyes.

"I'm Meera," she says. "Attorney Meera Fabregas."

Attorney. That figures.

There's a precision and a certainty to her, even in her shaken state. A steadiness that reminds me of people who had to learn how to stand back up.

I offer my hand, a gesture that's supposed to be safe, polite. "It's nice to meet you."

Her palm is small in mine, but her skin feels warm. Her grip is firm despite the tremor still in her fingers. I let go first, because I always do.

"It's nice to meet you, too," she says. "Thanks for your help."

"I'm sorry I wasn't able to reach him earlier," I reply. "I could have caught him before he did that to you."

She studies me closely, curiously, eyes cutting through adrenaline and courtesy. "Have you been…watching me?"

The question lands exactly where it should.

I could lie. Say it was a coincidence. Or maybe luck.

Instead, I answer, "Yes."

Her brows lift slightly.

"I wanted to make sure you were safe," I continue. "From the first day."

She doesn't step back. She doesn't accuse me of anything.

Meera just nods once, as if the answer fits something she already suspected.

I offer to walk her back to her pension house. She accepts without hesitation.

We take the boardwalk, beach on one side, town lights blinking on the other. Her steps are measured.

"Why September?" she asks quietly.

The question presses into me, slowly yet relentlessly.

"It's my wife's birthday yesterday," I say after a long pause. "She passed away almost two years ago. Cancer."

Facts first. Always facts.

"I came here because this place was her favorite view. We had our honeymoon in a resort nearby. She used to say sunsets made her believe in happy endings. Riding off into the sunset, all that." I swallow. "She owned a flower shop."

Meera stops. I stop too.

"My fiancé loved sunsets, too," she says. "He…he died in a crash. I work in the city, but I come back for his birthday. This is his hometown. And the pier was where he proposed to me."

Two stories. Different details. Same wound.

"I'm sorry for your loss," I say.

"I'm sorry for your loss, too," she answers. "Your wife sounds like a wonderful lady."

"You could say she was a romantic," I say, and feel it everywhere.

Meera smiles. It's soft and sad at the same time. "She's right. We didn't get our happy endings, but sunsets do make you believe in them. They're always something to look forward to, in spite of everything."

"They're like second chances, I guess," I murmur.

"You can say that," she says. "I believe in second chances. Maybe that's why I became a lawyer."

Neither of us say anything for a while, then she takes a deep breath and continues.

"Years ago, a very good friend of mine was killed in a robbery. His brother found the men who did it and finished them all off. I knew he did what he did out of love, so I did everything I could to make sure he got out of prison early. He and his wife have a son now. She's going to take the Bar exams next year. Hopefully she'll become a lawyer too."

I reach for her without thinking, tilting her chin gently.

"I've never heard anything more romantic than that," I tell her, "coming from a lawyer."

She laughs, blushing, seemingly surprised. "Look at us. Old romantics."

I step closer.

Because I know I want more of this.

I want to see myself reflected in someone else's grief and choosing not to look away.

And I know I want her.

Meera.

When I kiss her, it's careful.

An offering. A question.

And she answers.

Her mouth is warm and insistent. The spark catches fast, bright and hot. I groan in response, one hand cradling her cheek, the other going around her slender waist to pull her closer. She grips my shirt tightly, as though she needs something solid to hold onto.

"Do you want to come with me?" she asks breathlessly. "For coffee?"

"Yes," I say.

And for the first time in a long while, the word doesn't feel like a promise I can't keep.

CHAPTER 3

ANOTHER LIFE

MY LEGS DON'T STOP SHAKING, EVEN WHEN WE REACH my room at the pension house.

My fingers fumble the keys, but his hand covers mine, steady and firm, guiding the door open. He reaches up to flip on the light, a soft golden glow settling over the tiny space.

Inside, it feels too quiet. Too small. My pulse won't slow.

I set my bag down on the table, my breath still ragged.

I turn and look at him standing at the threshold—the buttons at his collar undone, the storm still raging in his eyes—and I realize exactly what I feel.

It's something I haven't felt in years. Something I never gave myself the permission to feel again.

It's want. It's need.

And it's the last thing from coffee.

Because it's him.

The door clicks shut behind him, and suddenly it's just us and the sound of the sea, muffled through the open window.

The words escape before I can stop them.

"I don't want to be alone tonight, Brian."

His silence is heavy, eyes locking onto mine. Then he steps closer, close enough that I feel his heat.

"Neither do I."

The kiss is molten, a clash of everything unsaid, a dam of the years breaking wide open.

His mouth claims mine with burning heat, his hands anchoring my waist. I gasp against him, and he deepens it, tongue sliding past my lips, tasting me.

I clutch at his shirt, feeling the solid muscle beneath, the tension coiled and breaking free. He lifts me easily, settling me on the edge of the bed without breaking the kiss.

"Meera," he murmurs against my throat. His hand slides down my arm, to my waist, pausing as if to ask permission. "Tell me if you want this. If not, I'll leave."

"Yes," I answer, arching into his touch. "I want this. I want you."

I shiver as he starts to bare my body, not just the skin but the parts of myself I've hidden for years. He pauses, eyes dark as he takes in the sight of my breasts, still partially covered by my lace bra.

"You're beautiful, Meera," he says, as if it's the simplest truth.

My throat tightens. I don't remember the last time anyone looked at me this way.

He undresses me slowly, kissing each new stretch of skin.

When his palm cups my bare breasts then moves to the heat between my legs, and when his mouth follows, I gasp out his name again and again, clutching his shoulders.

He doesn't stop there. His lips trail fire on my skin, then he slides lower, pushing my legs apart.

"You're so beautiful," he says again, voice gravelly with desire. "I want to taste all of you."

"Brian…" My eyes widen, and I almost scream when his mouth finds me.

But he is as steady as the tide.

His tongue and lips move relentlessly over that achingly wet part of me, flicking and swirling in maddening rhythm. His fingers follow, and I come undone, legs shooting into the air as he licks me clean, even as I shake and whimper under his touch.

His clothes come off then, one piece at a time. His body is warm and bronze, hard with muscle and discipline. In contrast, mine is soft, pale, trembling with need.

The contrast feels electric.

I trace the lines of his chest, his back, the ridges of strength I've only imagined. He shivers under my touch. Boldly, I reach for him, too, with both hands, rubbing and stroking the rigid length between my palms.

When he finally enters me, it's slow and tender, a stretch that steals my breath. He holds still, forehead pressed to mine, waiting.

"Okay?" he whispers.

"Yes," I whisper back, wrapping my legs around his hips, taking him deeper into me.

He moves carefully, each thrust measured, as if he's

determined not to break me. But soon his control melts into hunger, and the rhythm deepens. Our bodies find a pace that feels like waves—rolling, building, crashing.

I cling to him, nails in his back, gasping with every surge. He groans into my ear, muttering my name, growling and groaning as he comes apart in my arms.

It's not just sex.

It's choosing life again, together, in the dark of a seaside hotel.

When release finally takes me, it rips through me like a tidal wave.

He follows, holding me tightly, as if I'll drift away if he doesn't.

"Meera," he murmurs into my ear as we both ease down from the high of our shared pleasure. "Stay. Stay with me."

"Yes," I answer. "Yes."

CHAPTER 4

ANOTHER BEGINNING

MORNING COMES SLOWLY.

Not the kind that crashes in with light and noise, but the kind that seeps in. It's soft gray slipping through the thin curtains, the sea breathing somewhere beyond the walls.

I wake up before I mean to, the way I always do, trained by years of early calls and worse mornings.

She's still here.

Meera is curled against my chest, one arm draped over my ribs, her cheek warm where it rests against my skin. My arm is around her without memory of when I put it there, heavy and instinctive, as if my body decided something before my mind caught up.

For one suspended breath, fear tightens my chest.

I've known too many mornings that start like this, full

and whole with a dream, only to empty out in the next blink of reality.

Loss trains you for disappearance. It teaches you not to trust stillness.

She stirs. Her lashes flutter, and when her eyes open, they find mine without hesitation. There's no distance in her gaze.

"Good morning," I rasp out, voice still rough with sleep and something I don't want to admit to myself yet.

Her face breaks into a smile so open it almost hurts to look at. "Good morning."

Warmth floods me. Relief first, then something brighter. Something dangerously close to joy.

"You stayed," I say, and hear the question in it even if I didn't mean to put one there.

She props herself up on my chest, hair spilling over her bare shoulders, eyes steady and sure. She nudges her nose against mine. "Of course I stayed."

Of course.

The words lodge deeply.

My thumb finds her cheek, tracing slow circles as if I need to convince myself she's real, that this isn't another fever dream. She leans into the touch, eyes drooping.

I glance toward the window. Dawn is breaking, the horizon pale and tentative, seemingly asking for permission to glow.

"We've been chasing sunsets," I murmur. "Chasing ghosts."

My wife. Her fiancé. The lives we loved and lost, the

rituals we kept so we wouldn't forget who we were before the world took that part of us away.

"Maybe it's time to try something else."

She studies me, brow creasing slightly. "Like what?"

The words come carefully. I've spent years choosing them that way.

"What if we watched the sunrise together instead?" I say. "A new day. A new start."

Her breath catches. Tears gather in her eyes, then slip down her cheeks slowly even as she smiles.

"Yes," she says softly. "I'd like that very much."

Something in me settles then. A quiet kind of resolve that doesn't need grand declarations.

I kiss her gently, brushing away her tears with my thumb.

This kiss isn't fire. It isn't even hunger, although I want nothing more than to take her in my arms again and stay in this bed until sunset reaches us.

I kiss her with certainty.

With promise.

When we step out onto the balcony hand in hand, the sea opens before us, endless and patient. The horizon blooms with light then, gold bleeding into blue.

The world begins again, without apology.

I stand beside her, feeling the morning air on my skin, her fingers laced through mine.

For the first time in a long while, I'm not looking back.

This light isn't a farewell.

It's a welcome.

ABOUT THE AUTHOR

Shirley Siaton writes edgy and evocative novels and poems. Her worlds are in a deliciously dark cross-section of the romance, neo-noir, action, contemporary, and fantasy genres. Her background in various Asian martial arts inspires a lot of her work.

She has several books of fiction and poetry released since February 2023. Her first book is the free verse collection *Black Cat and other poems. Befallen* (March 2025) is her first full-length novel. She also pens juvenile literature as Shirley Parabia.

She is an award-winning writer, poet, and journalist in English, Filipino, and Hiligaynon. Her essays, short stories, and poems have been published internationally in print and digital media. Her multi-lingual plays have been staged in the Philippines.

Shirley is a black belt in Shotokan Karate and an international certified fitness coach. She has a Master's degree in Public Administration and works in education, wellness, and publishing. Originally from Iloilo City, she lives in the Middle East with her husband and two daughters.

ON THE WEB

Shirley's official website:
shirleysiaton.com

Complete reading guide:
shirley.pub

Subscribe to Shirley's VIP list for free exclusive updates:
newsletter.shirleysiaton.com

www.ingramcontent.com/pod-product-compliance
Lightning Source LLC
Chambersburg PA
CBHW021325060726
47591CB00006B/1869